DEEP IN THE JUNGLE

GERRY GRIFFITHS

SEVERED PRESS
HOBART TASMANIA

DEEP IN THE JUNGLE

DEDICATION

For my brother, Steve

1

A scream from the other side of the village woke Diogo, but he was uncertain if the sound had been real. His spirit soul was somewhere outside his body. He vaguely remembered the shaman's offering and drinking the brew that drove the demons forcefully, spewing out of him at both ends. The tremors had finally stopped, leaving him weak, but at least his body was rid of the parasites.

His lips were chapped and cracked, his throat raw. The jungle heat pulled at his pores, leaving his brown skin caked white with dried sweat. As his spirit soul returned and he became more himself, he dangled one leg out of the hammock.

The shellbacks of the scurrying cockroaches brushed the bottoms of his toes and the sole of his foot.

Another scream pierced the night.

A slant of moonlight shined inside his hut through the arched doorway. He could see the edge of the jungle but could not hear it, which he found strange and alarming. The jungle always spoke to him—why not tonight?

Swinging his other leg over the edge of the netting, Diogo attempted to stand. As soon as his feet touched the ground, his knees buckled but not enough to fall. He clung to the hammock, waiting for the swooning to leave his head.

Diogo looked down and watched the scavenging horde flitting between and over his feet. Whenever he would wake in the night and look down, the roaches were going in all directions, seeking food.

Tonight, they were clearly running away in one direction.

He shuffled toward the doorway, shoving the insects aside rather than squashing them with his bare feet.

A man yelled from nearby. Then, a woman screamed.

Diogo staggered out of his hut and looked out at the moonlit clearing in the center of the ring of huts. Villagers were running out of their thatched dwellings, shouting hysterically and screaming.

Giant spirit animals were attacking his people.

They were bigger than a man and walked on six legs.

He watched in horror as one stood up on its two hind legs and grabbed a frightened native woman with its other four appendages. It pulled her close in a lover's embrace and bit off her head at the neck with its razor-sharp jaws.

One of the creatures ran toward the jungle, carrying a crying baby in its mouth.

Some of the men had armed themselves with spears and knives, but the weapons were unable to penetrate the heavily armored skin of the intruders. Diogo could only watch as his village was overrun and his people were slaughtered.

The monsters that weren't pinning their victims to the ground and slashing apart their bodies were carrying ravaged chunks in their jaws and marching single file through a tunneled path carved in the vegetation.

Diogo heard something behind him and looked up.

Two of the black abominations were on the dome roof of his hut, looking down at him.

With new energy—and an immense desire to stay alive—Diogo dashed into the jungle, praying the evil spirits wouldn't follow.

2

Frank Travis looked at Wanda seated next to him. She was taking a nap, and understandably so. They'd been in the air for almost ten hours. It had been dark when they departed the Mineta San Jose International Airport and it would be dark by the time they arrived at the Eduardo Gomes International Airport in Manaus, Brazil, given the advanced three-hour time difference.

Convincing Wanda that Amazonas was the perfect place for their honeymoon had been a hard sell. Frank was sure it would be a week they would never forget, full of adventure with gorgeous landscapes and memories they would cherish for years to come.

Wanda had balked at first, citing she couldn't just pack up and leave her town without a sheriff. But then she did have a new deputy, and after some persuasion, she finally agreed Prospect would get by just fine despite her absence.

He knew that wasn't the real reason for her not wanting to come—it wasn't easy for someone who hated bugs with a passion to up and marry an entomologist. But then, didn't a lot of folks have strange bedfellows? Opposites attract, and all that.

Relationships these days were always complicated, especially when they involved marrying a woman with three kids of her own who had been graciously included in the honeymoon package.

Frank glanced across the aisle.

Ryan was in the aisle seat, reading the same in-flight magazine for the umpteenth time. Recently out of high school, he had entered a carpentry apprentice program. When he told his foreman he had an opportunity to go to Brazil, his boss was more than happy to give Ryan the week off as the young man had proved to be a fast learner, was a dedicated worker, and by all counts was going to be a promising tradesman.

In the middle seat was Ally. She'd be a high school senior after the summer was over. Being athletic and a star runner on the track team, she was looking forward to hiking the jungle trails. She had her eyes closed, listening to music through her earbuds.

Seven-year-old Dillon was in the third seat, gazing out the window at the fluffy white clouds and lush greenery below. He had been genuinely excited about the trip as he thought Frank's job, teaching college students about bugs at UC Davis, was the coolest thing ever.

The pilot's voice sounded over the address system. They would be landing in the next ten minutes. Manaus was 82 degrees with humidity of 84%.

Frank figured after they claimed their bags and spent time standing outside waiting for a taxi, their clothes would be wet rags.

He gently nudged Wanda awake.

"Are we there?" she asked, blinking her eyes.

"Almost."

Wanda turned and looked out her window. "Is that an oil slick?"

"Let me see," Frank said, scooting over so he could see what Wanda was looking at.

Below was a large river, the length of its surface divided roughly up the middle by brown silty water on one side and water the color of dark tea on the other, like two liquids incapable of mixing.

"They're actually two different rivers sources that flow beside each other for miles but never actually blend as one," Frank explained. "The Rio Negro and the Rio Salimoes. Together they form the Amazon River. The phenomenon is called the Meeting of the Waters."

"Like water and oil."

"Somewhat."

"Look at the beautiful sunset," Wanda said, as she took Frank's hand and pulled him in close so they could enjoy the distant view together as the dark blue sky bruised purple and the orange crown of the sun dipped into the horizon.

Wanda was an attractive woman in her mid-forties, and Frank was deeply in love with her even though she wasn't overly affectionate, which he attributed to not having male companionship for a number of years. That is, until they met a year ago.

But perhaps that was all about to change. As at the moment, Wanda showed no sign of wanting to let go of Frank's hand. Frank decided to put all of his personal fears aside and just go with the flow.

This might prove to be a great vacation after all.

3

Frank could see everyone was clearly exhausted when they arrived at the low-budget hotel and knew he had made the right choice by not further extending their traveling until the next day. After checking in at the desk, the family traipsed up the stairs to the second floor where they had booked two adjacent rooms.

It had been previously decided Wanda and Ally would share a room while Frank and the boys bunked together.

When Frank unlocked both doors and everyone looked inside their rooms, they saw the accommodations were sparse with no amenities whatsoever. No televisions, WiFi, or radios. Just single size beds for each occupant, and a small table and a chair in each room.

There was no air conditioning, only an overhead fan with a single light bulb and a window that had been left open to allow some airflow into the tiny spaces.

The plan was to use the hotel as a stopover and get a good night's sleep. After breakfast the family would continue their trip and board a riverboat that would take them on a four-hour journey down the Amazon River to a jungle resort where they would spend the remainder of their stay.

"Certainly not the Hilton," Wanda quipped.

"No, but it's clean," Frank said. "And no bed bugs," he added with some assurance.

Wanda shot him a skeptical look.

"Maybe I shouldn't have said that."

"Maybe is right," Wanda said, scratching her arm as if Frank had just sent her a subliminal message.

Ally went into the room, dropped her bag on the floor and flopped onto one of the beds.

Ryan and Dillon dragged their wheeled duffels into the other room and parked them inside the doorway. Frank came in and tossed his travel bag on the bed by the window. "So what do you guys think?" he asked. "Pretty bare bones, eh?"

"It's not so bad," Dillon said, already digging into his bag and pulling out a worn DC Kids Comic.

Ryan took out his smartphone and checked it for reception. "Good thing I have satellite," he said and smiled.

"Believe me, after everyone's gotten some rest and is fresh tomorrow, there's going to be so much to do, you two are going to forget about all these distractions."

Neither Ryan nor Dillon commented. Ryan was too busy flipping through his favorites while Dillon's nose was glued to another Batman adventure.

The overhead fan did little to cool the room, as it was still stifling from having been closed up during the day.

Frank went over, looked out the window, and saw a small courtyard and a fountain below, lit up by tiny lights strung between two palm trees. He could hear the songfest of the katydids as the bush crickets rubbed their forewings together to either allure a mate or ward off aggressors.

He took a deep breath and could smell the river. It had been nearly three years since he had been back in the Amazon. He suddenly realized how much he had missed being here. He hoped Wanda would give the place a chance during their vacation.

That's when he heard Wanda and Ally yell.

Frank bolted into the hall and ran into the next room. "What is it? What's wrong?"

Wanda and Ally had backed into a corner of the room. Ally was pointing at something big, crawling slowly across the blanket on the bed by the window.

"Frank! What the hell is that?" Wanda shouted.

He took another step in the room for a closer look.

Ryan and Dillon rushed to the doorway but didn't venture further when they saw the thing on the bed.

"That's a Goliath birdeater."

"Are you serious? That thing eats birds?" Wanda said.

"So it's been said. Some call it the chicken-eating spider."

Dillon walked slowly into the room and stood next to Frank. "Can we catch it?"

"Dilly, you'll do no such thing," Wanda said adamantly.

The brown tarantula stopped moving as if sensing it had become a main attraction. Its body was the size of a guava fruit and had a leg span of almost ten inches.

Frank thought better than to mention they were looking at a species of spider that was the biggest in the world, as he didn't want to freak everyone out, especially Wanda, who at the moment looked like she was about to come unglued.

"Here, I'll take it outside."

"You're not going to kill it?" Wanda said.

"Heavens no." Frank went over to the bed.

"Be careful," Ally warned.

Wanda put her arm around her daughter. "Frank? Are you sure? Isn't it poisonous?"

"No more than a wasp sting."

Frank put his hand on the blanket and lightly drummed his fingers to coax the spider, which stepped slowly up onto his palm. "Must weigh a good six ounces."

"Can I hold it?" Dillon asked, putting both hands out.

"You can touch it, but don't frighten it."

"Don't frighten it? What about us?" Wanda said.

Dillon stroked the spider's back. "This is so cool."

"Come on. Let's go downstairs and put her outside."

"What, that's a female?" Wanda asked with alarm.

"Don't worry, she's not pregnant." Frank didn't elaborate that female Goliath birdeaters could lay up to two hundred eggs at one time and had a lifespan of up to twenty-five years, which added up to a ton of spiderlings.

Frank pulled the drawer completely out from the small table to use as a carrying box and set the spider inside. "Ryan, can you grab something I can place over the top?"

Ryan ran out into the hall and came back with a towel he had taken from the communal bathroom shared by all the residents on the second floor.

"Perfect." Frank draped the towel over the drawer. He didn't want to risk carrying the giant spider in his hand and have another tourist come out of their room and panic, scaring the creature.

Frank and Dillon were starting for the door when suddenly the floor beneath their feet began to tremble and the room shook. Wanda and Ally swayed but managed to stay on their feet as Ryan braced himself against the doorjamb.

"I think we just had an earthquake," Frank said, the drawer in one hand as he held on to Dillon.

"My God, what next?" Wanda said.

"We'll be right back," Frank said as he and Dillon left the room.

As they went down the stairs, Frank could hear voices throughout the small hotel, people reacting to the tremor.

Once outside, Frank and Dillon found a spot far enough away from the main entrance of the hotel and released the large spider under a broad-leaf fern.

Upon their return, they found Wanda and Ally down on the floor on their hands and knees, inspecting under the beds. Frank noticed the window was closed.

"Everyone okay?" he asked.

"Just peachy," Wanda replied. She got up and sat on the edge of the bed.

Ally stood and looked over at Ryan, who was staring at his smartphone. "Anything?"

"Here, in Manaus, it registered a magnitude of 1.5. The epicenter was four hundred miles away. There they think it was more like a 6.0."

"Oh my God," Wanda said.

"Lucky for us," Frank said. He put his hands together and looked about the room. "Well, maybe it's time we got some sleep. Tomorrow's going to be a full day."

"After an earthquake and finding a humongous spider in our room," Wanda said, "you really think we're going to be able to sleep?"

Frank gave everyone a weak smile. "Welcome to the Amazon."

4

Despite the chaotic night, everyone managed to finally drift off to sleep, and before they realized, it was dawn. There were other tourists occupying rooms on the same floor but judging by the Do Not Disturb signs on their doorknobs—Manaus being famous for its nightlife—it was doubtful if Frank and his family would have to fight for the communal bathroom so early in the morning.

Wanda and Ally were the first to use the showers. They were out in less than twenty minutes, surprising Frank and the boys, who were waiting impatiently out in the hall.

"That was fast," Frank said.

Wanda walked by Frank, her hair still dripping and adding to a damp spot on the back of her shirt. Her flip-flops sounding like sharp gunfire as she strode down the hall.

"There's no hot water," Wanda snapped. She made a quick turn and disappeared in her room.

"I'm sorry, I should have mentioned that."

Ally rolled her eyes at Frank and hurried after her mother.

Forty-five minutes later, after everyone had gotten dressed and packed up their bags, they went down to the small restaurant and had a basic breakfast consisting of *tapioquinha*, a fruit-filled pancake, along with muesli cereal, baked bread, papaya, and mozzarella cheese.

Ryan and Ally had orange juice, Dillon the chocolate powdered milk.

Frank and Wanda polished off a tall carafe of strong Brazilian coffee, which was a nice, rejuvenating way to start the day.

"So, how far to the boat dock?" Wanda asked, wiping her mouth with a paper napkin, no longer in a sour mood.

"About a thirty-minute drive." Frank looked at his watch. "In fact, the taxi should be arriving to pick us up right about now. Guys ready?"

***

The riverboat was a long dugout with a canvas roof painted the same dark green as the hull. Wooden bench seats ran along the insides, enough space to accommodate a dozen passengers. A single crewmember—a short, barefoot local in white shorts and a Nike emblem t-shirt—steered the craft, which clipped steadily along at twenty miles an hour, propelled by a noisy 65 hp Evinrude mounted on the transom.

It was a four-hour boat ride to their next destination: the Black Caiman Jungle Lodge and Resort.

Besides Frank and his family, there were five other passengers on board. During the first hour of the journey everyone took the time to get to know one another as they were all headed to the same resort.

The two sitting on the bench along with Frank, Wanda, and Dillon were Jackie Brice and Conroy Macklin. Conroy liked to be called Macky. They explained they were students on an extended field trip funded by their university.

Jackie's major was zoology; Macky's, ichthyology. When Dillon asked what that was, Macky flapped his hands in front of his ears like gills and made a guppy face. Dillon caught on right away and burst out laughing.

On the opposite side of the boat, Ryan had struck up a lengthy conversation with the student sitting to his right named Ben Turmain. He talked nonstop about his recent travels, which interested Ryan immensely.

Ally was getting to know James Donner and Kathy Beckerman, a couple with plans to marry once they earned their degrees. They spoke of their tree climbing experience the day before and how much they enjoyed it. James was a biology student with a minor in dendrology, which he further explained was the study of trees. Kathy's major was ornithology.

Halfway into the voyage, Macky pointed off the starboard side of the boat. "Hey, everyone, there's a pod of dolphins."

Dillon hung over the gunwale to get a better look.

"Careful there," Frank said, grabbing the back of Dillon's floatation vest before the boy fell overboard.

Six pink dorsal fins could be seen twenty feet off in the current.

The driver slowed the boat down to about ten miles per hour.

Macky gave the man an appreciative wave. He turned to the group and said, "Amazon river dolphins aren't particularly fast swimmers. Don't expect to see them diving across the bow like in videos."

"I always thought dolphins were gray," Wanda said.

"The young ones are," Macky said. "These turn pink as they gradually become adults."

"They sure are big fish," Dillon said.

"Well, they're really mammals. See their blowholes?"

"But I thought you knew all about fish?"

"And other things," Macky said, and then looked over at Frank.

"Dillon is very analytical," Frank said.

"What'd you call me?"

Macky reached over and patted Dillon on the knee. "I think your father said you are a lot like Mr. Spock, you know, on Star Trek."

Dillon's face lit up. "Cool."

5

Once the boat docked, everyone collected their backpacks and travel luggage and disembarked one at a time. They headed down the narrow wharf stretching over the shallow water to the shore where three lodge employees were waiting.

The head guide introduced himself as Ignacio. He was Brazilian-born and wore a clean white t-shirt with the lodge's name across the front, a pair of dark brown khakis, and hiking boots. A shock of black hair stuck out under the brim of a white ball cap also sporting the resort's emblem.

The two men standing on each side of Ignacio were Enzo and Murilo, who were identical twins. Their only distinguishing feature was their attire—atop bare feet and cargo shorts, Enzo was wearing a green work shirt and Murilo had on a blue one.

For five minutes Ignacio gave his well-rehearsed greeting, welcoming everyone to the Black Caiman Jungle Lodge and Resort and briefly touching on the highlights of the adventures in store for the week to come. Once he was through, Ignacio asked Frank and Wanda to follow him while Enzo assisted Ryan, Ally, and Dillon, and Murilo showed the college students to their accommodations.

The entire resort was raised on a stilts, twenty feet above the ground—Ignacio said it was necessary because of the floodwaters during the rainy season—with catwalks branching off from the main lodge, leading to the different guests' rooms.

Once they arrived at their quarters, Frank thanked Ignacio, who smiled and walked off down the railed catwalk.

"Don't expect it to be too fancy, but I think it will be comfortable," Frank said to Wanda as he held the door open.

She walked in and looked around the room. A sitting area in the corner had two high-back wicker chairs and end tables constructed of rattan with basket-weaved tops. Rafters crisscrossed eight feet above her head, the high-pitched thatch roof stretching another ten feet up to a peak. There was no air conditioning unit or even a ceiling fan.

Instead, there were two screen mesh windows on opposite walls to allow a cross breeze to cool the room, which at the moment had to be over 80 degrees.

After a moment studying the white mosquito netting suspended over the large four-post bed, Wanda turned to Frank. "I take it this is the honeymoon suite?"

"Well, what do you think?" he asked.

Wanda waltzed up to Frank, put her arms around his neck, and kissed him on the lips.

"I take it you approve."

"Let's just say—"

"Hey, there's a monkey in our room!" It was Ally's voice coming through the window from the guest room next door.

"Can I play with it?" Dillon asked.

"I don't know, maybe later," Ryan said. "Come on, out you get, shoo."

Wanda looked up at Frank, doing her best to keep a straight face, as they listened to the commotion next door; the jungle guest apparently reluctant to leave. "Maybe you should go over there."

"They'll sort it out," Frank said as he smiled and kissed his wife.

6

Ally couldn't believe she was actually doing this. She looked over the edge of the platform down through the trees to the ground, one hundred feet below. Half of her was scared to death but the other half was pumped. It was the same nervous rush she always got before exploding out of the blocks during a track meet.

While she adjusted the chinstrap on her helmet, Enzo was double checking her rigging. He cinched up her waist belt and made sure her harness was properly connected to the pulley.

"Is this your first time?" James asked Ally. He and Kathy were also geared up with helmets and harnesses as they stood by waiting their turn.

"Yes," she replied, trying to sound brave.

"Don't worry," James assured her. "Kathy and I have done this a few times. It's fairly safe."

"Fairly?" Ally said, unable to conceal the fear in her voice.

"Don't listen to him," Kathy piped in, elbowing James hard enough to make him step precariously close to the edge.

"Whoa, are you trying to kill me?" James said, even though there was no real threat of him falling as he was temporarily tethered to the massive tree trunk that the platform was built around.

Enzo patted Ally on the shoulder to signal he was through with his safety inspection and she was ready to go.

"Remember what we told you earlier. Use your dominant hand to brake," Kathy said.

Ally tugged on the wristbands of her double-layer leather gloves to make sure they were snug. She set her weight down on the harness's butt straps, reached as far back as she could with her right hand and grabbed the overhead cable, that hand being the one she would use to brake herself.

"Have fun," James said.

Ally leaned back and her feet left the platform as she sped down the zip line through the rainforest. She was actually gliding down on her back with her boots out in front. Her left hand held on tight to the lanyard connected to the pulley running down the cable, designed to prevent her from spinning during her descent.

At first she controlled her speed by over braking, then gradually eased up, allowing her momentum to build up. The cable whined loudly above her head. The faster she went, the louder it became, like the building intensity of a jet engine.

She gazed over the tips of her boots as the forest rushed at her, narrowly missing branches as she sped past tree trunks so close, she might have been able to reach out and touch them if she'd had a free hand. At the moment, she was too busy controlling her ride.

It was so incredible. She felt like a bird swooping through the jungle.

The thrill lasted for over a minute.

Soon the slack in the cable slowed her descent as she reached another platform at the end of the line where Murilo was waiting.

The guide helped her to stop so she could stand. He attached her safety tether and unhooked the pulley from the cable. "How was your trip?" he asked.

Ally gave him a big smile. "That was really fun."

She could hear James whooping it up as he barreled down the zip line.

Already, this was becoming a vacation she would never forget.

7

Even though Frank was confident and knew his way around the jungle, he thought as long as they were paying for the service, he should let Ignacio take them on a nature hike.

Ryan had asked if it was okay if he hung out with Ben, Jackie, and Macky as they had invited him to join them as they had separate plans. Wanda didn't see why not as Ally was off with James and Kathy spending the afternoon on the zip line.

It was important everyone had a good time. Ryan had developed a comradeship with the three since their arrival, and it was good for him to spend time with people his own age, not to mention what he might learn from the students.

The trail was well-trodden and the weather was hot. It wasn't so much the heat but the insufferable humidity that made it so unbearable. To keep away the mosquitoes, everyone wore long sleeve shirts and long pants to cover their skin, which only made them sweat more.

Frank could tell by Wanda's expression she was uncomfortable.

"You know, we can go back any time."

"It's no cooler back at the room. Besides, I think Dillon's having fun," Wanda replied. She wore a tan ranger hat with a neck shade. Sweat beaded her forehead.

Twenty minutes into their hike, Dillon exclaimed, "Look at the walking leaves."

The path was alive with hundreds of tiny pieces of green vegetation, marching across the dirt.

Ignacio stood next to the boy and looked down at the ground. "Those are leafcutter ants carrying bits of leaves they have chewed off the plant." He pointed toward a large mound of dirt not far from the trail. "That's their colony."

Dillon stooped to get a closer look.

"Be careful they don't crawl on you," Frank warned. "They do bite."

The boy was not afraid but moved back anyway. "Are they going to eat the leaves?"

"No, not exactly," Frank said. "They use the leaves to harvest fungi and eat that. And they're pretty strong. They can carry fifty times their own weight."

"Wow," Dillon said, truly amazed.

"That would be like you lifting your mother's car up over your head and carrying it down the street."

"Cool."

They walked on the outer edge of the path so as not to disturb the industrious ants and continued following Ignacio down the trail.

During their hike they encountered a young six-foot-long boa constrictor slithering through the debris. Ignacio didn't have any problem picking it up to show off the large snake.

"Would you like for me to put it on your shoulders?" Ignacio asked Wanda.

"Do what?"

"He won't let it hurt you," Frank said.

"All right. Snakes I don't mind," Wanda said.

Ignacio held onto the back of the snake's head and draped the body behind Wanda's neck. The tip of the serpent's tail slowly began to coil around her wrist. She moved her hand away so she could feel its thick body.

"It's heavier than I would have imagined."

Frank pulled out his camera and took a picture.

Dillon was excited. "Gosh, Mom. You look like Sheena: Queen of the Jungle."

"Well, thank you, Dilly. I think," Wanda replied.

Ignacio lifted the big snake off of Wanda's shoulders. He carried it back to the same spot where he had found it and let it go.

A few minutes later, Dillon got his chance to hold a sloth. After some deliberation, Ignacio was able to untangle the animal from a low hanging branch. The brown-furred animal was around fifteen pounds and had long curved claws that looked lethal. The guide assured Wanda the claws were not used as weapons but rather so the sloth could hang effortlessly from tree branches.

As soon as Ignacio put the sloth against Dillon's chest, the creature wrapped its long arms around the boy.

Frank smiled. "I think he likes you."

The sloth took its time to turn his head and looked at Frank.

"How come it moves so slow?" Dillon asked.

"Sloths have a very slow metabolism as they only eat leaves, which take longer for their stomachs to digest, so they have less energy. They process food so slow, they only have to go to the bathroom once a week."

"Once a week? I couldn't hold it a week!" Dillon said.

"What's even stranger is they come down to the ground to do their business. Even dig a hole and bury it. Much like a housecat."

"That's weird."

For being a wild animal just plucked out of a tree, the sloth seemed content to be treated as a trusted pet and held by Dillon.

This time, Wanda took the picture with her smartphone.

***

"So, do you fish much at home?" Macky asked, sitting near the bow of the canoe provided by the resort, holding on to the end of his bamboo pole.

"There's a lake not too far from where we live. Catfish and trout mostly," Ryan replied. He sat near the stern, watching his line in the murky water and anxiously waiting for a strike. They were about half an hour away from the lodge and had found a cove to fish.

The tip of Ryan's thin rod dipped into the water.

"There you go," Macky said.

Ryan pulled up on his fishing pole, the end still under the surface. "Putting up a pretty good fight."

"It's their aggressive nature."

Lifting steadily so as not to snap the line, Ryan managed to pop the small fish out of the water. At first glance, it looked like a crappie, a fish he might have caught back home. He swung the fish into the middle of the boat.

Macky leaned his pole against the gunwale and reached over, grabbing the fish thrashing in the boat. "You have to be careful. One good bite, and they can take off a finger."

Ryan watched Macky grip the fish firmly just behind the gills and carefully pry the hook out of its mouth. A small piece of meat was still on the barbs.

The piranha snapped at the bait like a ferocious attack dog.

"Whoa," Ryan said, awestruck at the fish's viciousness. He couldn't take his eyes off the razor-sharp teeth.

"They have incredibly strong jaws. Those teeth have no other purpose than to rip flesh."

The upper and lower rows of teeth were set closely together, each tooth looking like it had been filed to a sharp tip.

"Actually, piranhas are essential to this ecosystem," Macky explained. "That's because they eat anything, dead or alive. Helps to reduce decay matter in the water."

"Tell me they don't get any bigger than this," Ryan said, his fish being close to four inches in length.

"Try ten inches long. Swim into a school that size, and they'd strip you to the bone in a matter of minutes." Macky offered the fish to Ryan. "You want to keep it?"

"Nah, but let me get a picture." Ryan took out his smartphone and took a few photos. "You can let it go."

Macky smiled and dropped the fish over the side. "Good. Catch and release, I like that."

"I don't think I'll be in the mood for fish for awhile after looking at that ugly mug."

"That's too bad."

"What do you mean?"

"You didn't see the main entree for tonight's dinner?"

"No," Ryan said. "What are we having?"

"Grilled piranha."

8

A massive round mahogany table took up most of the main dining room. Frank, Wanda, and Dillon were seated together. Ally sat between James and Kathy. Next to her were Ben, then Ryan, Jackie, and Macky. The smaller tables against the walls were all vacant, Ignacio anticipating the arrival of more guests in a week's time.

Stylish candelabras on the tabletop offered suitable lighting, giving the culinary hut a warm ambience. There were ice water pitchers and uncorked bottles of wine on the table. The room was decorated with jungle art and detailed wooden sculptures of black jaguars and ebony caiman. Two blue macaws were perched on swings in an airy cage at the entryway.

Enzo and Murilo were subbing as waiters, transporting serving platters in from the kitchen. They were also the cooks and the housekeepers as the rest of the staff wasn't due to report for work until the next batch of guests arrived.

The first entree was shrimp bobo, a split pea-looking chowder made from pureed shrimp mixed with coconut milk, served with baskets of freshly baked bread and little porcelain cups filled with *requeijao*, which was like a salty cream cheese.

For the next course, Enzo brought in dishes of already sliced portions of polenta, a cornmeal that looked like sausage. Murilo came into the dining room, pushing a cart with bowls of rice, beans, and chayote squashes.

Enzo returned to the kitchen with his cart and came out wheeling two large serving platters, one with succulent browned chicken breasts just off the grill.

Macky grinned as he looked over at Ryan. "Bon appetite."

"You weren't kidding," Ryan said, staring at the mound of grilled piranha on the other platter.

"Be careful, as the teeth are very, very sharp," Enzo warned everyone.

Wanda forked a fish, put it on her dish, and sliced off the head. She slid the rest onto Dillon's plate. "Watch for bones."

"Can I keep the head?"

"I don't think so."

"Why not?"

"Better eat, before your food gets cold."

Dillon picked up his fork and dove in, his plate already filled with rice and beans.

Ryan took a bite of fish and looked over at Macky. "Not bad, but I think I'll stick to trout."

"An acquired taste, eh?"

"You might say that." Ryan took the time to scrape the meat off the tiny skeleton and got maybe two forkfuls; a lot of work for nothing, like cracking open crab legs and only getting a few strips of meat.

Everyone delved in, preparing their plates, passing bowls and platters to the person sitting next to them.

Ben cut a slice of chicken and popped it in his mouth then turned to Ryan. "How would you like to join Jackie and me and go see an indigenous tribe?"

"When?"

"Tomorrow."

"I don't know what we have scheduled," Ryan said.

"You should," Jackie piped in. "You'd find it really interesting. Besides, we'll only be gone two days."

"I'd have to ask." Ryan glanced over at his mother. "Mom?"

Wanda had been listening as she ate and now turned her full attention to her son. "Where is the tribe located?"

"It's near the Vale do Javari Indigenous Territory," Ben said. "About a four-hour flight from here."

Wanda looked at Frank; she had no idea where that was.

"I'm familiar with that area. It's usually restricted to outside tourists."

"We have special permission," Ben said. "As well as the proper inoculation documents. Does Ryan have his?"

"Yes, we all had to have vaccines before we traveled down here."

"How are you planning to get there?" Frank asked.

"Floatplane," Ben replied. "Our pilot is Miles Gifford."

"I know Miles. He's a damn good bush pilot."

"So, can I go?" Ryan asked.

"What do you think, Frank? Is it safe?" Wanda asked unable to mask the concern in her voice.

Frank returned his attention back to Ben. "I take it you're visiting the Matis."

"Yes, sir."

"If it's okay with his mother, I don't see why not. They're a very generous people and I think Ryan would find it interesting."

"Thanks, Frank," Wanda said under her breath.

Frank turned and leaned in close. "Sorry, I didn't mean to put you on the spot."

"Well, I'm trusting you."

"It's a once in a lifetime experience."

Wanda turned to her son. "Sure, Ryan, you can go."

"Thanks Mom," Ryan said.

Looking at both Ben and Jackie, Wanda said, "Make sure nothing happens to my boy."

"Mom, please," Ryan said, cringing in his seat.

"We will," Jackie said and grinned at Ryan.

"Great, after dessert, you can come over to our bungalow and we'll show you what to bring," Ben said. "We'll be leaving before daybreak."

Enzo and Murilo came back into the dining room, both pushing separate serving carts. Enzo's held carafes filled with hot Brazilian coffee, and Murilo's had lemon pastries, cupcakes with brown sprinkles, two bowls with whipped cream and strawberries, a plate of sugar cones, and a scoop. There were also small cups filled with vanilla ice cream and a fifth bottle of Kahlua, a liqueur derived from the coffee bean and alcohol for a topping.

Frank clinked his spoon against his wineglass, stood, and raised his glass in a toast.

Everyone picked up their glasses and turned to Frank.

"I would like to thank my lovely bride, Wanda, for agreeing to come on this crazy adventure." He gazed down at Wanda, who looked up at him and smiled.

"To my family and our new friends!"

"Here, here," everyone cheered.

Frank sat down and finished off his wine. He switched beverages and poured himself a cup of coffee.

Ally, James, and Kathy were taking turns building sugar cones with whipped cream and strawberries.

"If it's okay, Mom, I'm going to see what I need to put together for tomorrow," Ryan said, standing up from the table. Ben and Jackie had already gotten up and were tucking their chairs in.

"Am I going to see you before you leave?" Wanda asked.

Ryan looked at Ben and Jackie.

They both shook their heads.

"I guess not," he replied.

"Then come here and give me a kiss goodbye," Wanda said.

Ryan went over to his mom and Wanda gave him a big kiss on the cheek. He gave her a hug.

"Now you be careful."

"I will."

"We want to hear all about it when you get back," Frank said, patting Ryan on the shoulder.

"Night." Ryan rushed off, catching up to Ben and Jackie who were already leaving the dining room.

Wanda looked at Frank. "Am I silly to worry?"

"No. He'll be fine. You want a sugar cone?"

"No, I think I'd like the ice cream cup."

"Sure," Frank said. He reached across the table and grabbed two cups, along with the bottle of liqueur.

"And heavy on the Kalula, please," Wanda said, still gazing at the entryway even though Ryan had already gone.

9

Ryan silenced the alarm on his cell phone and climbed out of bed. He'd laid out his clothes the night before so as not to waste time. He quickly dressed in a long-sleeve shirt and put on trousers with elastic ankle bands to prevent bugs from crawling up his pant legs.

He made sure he was quiet as possible so as not to wake Ally and Dillon, who were still fast asleep in their beds under the white mosquito netting that protected them from the malaria-carrying pests. The netting also served as room dividers for privacy.

It was still dark so he used the flashlight feature on his phone so he could see to lace his boots. Next to him lay his daypack. Inside were a change of underwear and socks, a baseball cap, sunglasses, a first aid kit, a spray bottle of insect repellant, a toothbrush and eco-friendly toothpaste, a sealed plastic bag containing his inoculation papers and his passport, and a liter of drinking water.

He'd also packed an extra Dri-Fit shirt made of synthetic material, instead of a cotton shirt, because once the natural fabric became damp from perspiration it wouldn't dry properly due to the high humidity, and there was nothing worse than walking around all day in a damp shirt.

He crept out of the bungalow and quietly closed the door behind him.

Ben and Jackie were waiting for him with flashlights at the end of the catwalk.

"The plane should be here at first light," Ben said, taking the lead as they headed down the walkway.

Rays of sunlight began filtering down through the trees, so they put away their flashlights.

They reached the wharf and walked onto the dock stretching out over the brown, silt-rich water.

Soon, Ryan heard the drone of a distant airplane. Gazing up at the flamingo-colored sky, he saw the navigation lights of a small aircraft as it made its descent and the two pontoons splashed down. The single-engine floatplane skimmed down the center of the river and, after reducing its speed, taxied over. The pilot shut off the engine as the plane drifted up to the end of the boat dock.

Ben reached out and grabbed a strut under the belly connected to one of the pontoons to temporarily moor the plane.

The pilot, Miles Gifford, pushed the side door open. "Morning everyone. Climb aboard." He wore a brown leather bomber jacket, Ray-Bans, and khakis. An unlit stogy was wedged in the corner of his mouth and looked like a permanent fixture, like a cowboy with a blade of grass.

Jackie stepped up first and climbed into the seat directly behind the pilot. Ryan got in and sat in the seat next to Jackie. They put their bags on the two seats behind them while Ben got in and closed the door. He sat in the copilot's seat.

"I see you brought a guest," Miles said to Ben and Jackie.

"This is Ryan Rafferty," Jackie said, making the introduction.

"Nice to meet you, son," Miles said and shook Ryan's hand.

"You, too," Ryan said. He looked about the cockpit and passenger interior, never before having been in an aircraft of this type. "What kind of plane is this?" he asked the pilot.

"You're sitting in a de Havilland DHC-2 Beaver, built in 1967. She's a single prop with a Pratt and Whitney 450-horsepower engine, cruising speed around 150 miles per hour. Normal range is 450 miles but as I often take clients on long hauls, such as what we will be doing today, I've made some modifications and added a larger fuel tank. She may not purr like a kitten but she's one reliable bird. Harrison Ford has one of these."

"You mean the Star Wars actor?" Ryan asked.

"One and the same. Better buckle up. There's headphones on the armrest," Miles said and faced the controls.

Ryan put on his headset and cinched up his seatbelt.

As soon as Miles started the powerful engine and the propeller began to spin, Ryan could feel the vibration coursing through his body.

Miles reached up and made adjustments to one of the throttles on the console on the dashboard. By the way he kept fiddling with the lever, Ryan guessed he was controlling the mixture, as each time he moved it, the engine would run marginally smoother.

Miles wrote in a small three-ring binder, then closed it up and stuffed the notebook in a side compartment on his door. He checked the dials and gauges, made a few calibrations, then throttled forward, putting both hands on the yoke which was attached to another similar-looking stick in front of Ben, seated in the copilot's seat.

Ryan looked out his side window and watched as they sped across the water. Before he knew it, they were airborne and he was looking down at the treetops as the floatplane flew over the interior of the rainforest.

"Bet you never thought you would be doing this," Jackie's voice said into Ryan's headset.

He looked to his left and saw Jackie smiling at him.

Ryan grinned back. He gave her a thumbs up. For the first time, he wondered if Jackie and Ben were in a relationship. He had never seen them act like boyfriend and girlfriend.

He liked the idea of getting to know Jackie better.

The last time he was this excited, he'd just bought his '71 Pontiac Firebird Trans Am. Oh, how he loved that car. He settled back in his seat and gazed out his window at the misty cloud cover hovering over the rainforest.

In just a few short hours, he and the others would be landing in a place few people were ever allowed to go, and he would actually be getting to meet a reclusive tribe of Amazonian Indians.

Sure beat Disney World.

10

Wanda couldn't believe how hard the rain was coming down as she watched the deluge through the dining room window. It was like they had suddenly been hit by a typhoon. A stand of water had quickly accumulated down near some of the pillars supporting a nearby catwalk. The rain was so forceful, it looked like the surface of the large puddle was being pelted by machinegun fire.

"Never rains like this at home," Wanda said to Frank sitting across from her at the table along with Ally and Dillon. They were having an early breakfast before starting their day.

"The rains here can be torrential but they don't last long," he said, taking a sip of his coffee. "It'll clear up soon and we can go for another hike."

"Can I go on the zip line?" Dillon asked, picking at a tapioca crepe with little enthusiasm.

"You're too little," Ally said. She was enjoying a piece of cheese bread.

"I'm tall enough to ride the Giant Dipper," he protested.

"A roller coaster is different."

"Not fair, you got to go."

Ally turned to Wanda. "Mom? Can you help me out here?"

"Dilly, your sister's right. The zip line is way too dangerous."

"Don't worry, Dillon," Frank jumped in. "Where we're going today, there will be plenty of danger."

"Really?" Dillon said, unable to contain his excitement.

Wanda gave Frank a concerned look.

He merely winked back.

When Wanda turned and looked out the window, the rain had already stopped.

***

Everyone wore ponchos because walking through the jungle after a heavy rainfall was similar to strolling through a building being doused by a sprinkler system. Water droplets continued to cascade from the treetops, funneling down large fronds and dripping off the leaves, though two-thirds of the moisture never reached the ground, evaporating back into the air to form the next barrage of rain clouds.

James, Kathy, and Macky had decided to come along, Enzo as the guide. Today, the native Brazilian was wearing a brown t-shirt under his partially unbuttoned raincoat. Wherever Murilo was, he was wearing a different color t-shirt so guests could tell them apart.

Twenty minutes into the hike, Enzo had everyone pause to observe a small short-legged rodent on the ground, biting into a grapefruit-size shell.

"That animal is an agouti," Enzo said. "It is good for the rainforest. It has strong teeth and can chew out the seed nuts. Those it doesn't eat, later makes for more trees."

"Brazilian nut trees can grow as tall as one hundred-sixty feet," James added, "and believe it or not, some have been around for a thousand years."

"That's really something," Wanda said, craning her neck to look up through the clustered trees.

"That seed pod the agouti is trying to crack probably weighs around five pounds. So imagine getting conked on the head."

"That would hurt," Ally said.

Kathy pointed at a low hanging branch just above their heads. "Hey everybody, take a look at that."

All eyes peered up at a tiny gray bird with a reddish-orange underbelly.

"That's a rufous-bellied thrush. It's actually Brazil's national bird."

A gathering of small green birds were perched on a single branch.

"Those are maroon-bellied parakeets," Kathy said knowledgably, sounding like a guide conducting a tour through an aviary.

Enzo waved the group on and everyone followed him down the trail.

They were coming up on a clearing when Enzo turned and put his finger up to his lips asking everyone to lower their voices. He pointed to a small group of animals feeding on patches of grass. They had short hair, some being over four feet long. The largest had to weigh over a hundred pounds.

"What are those?" Wanda whispered to Frank.

"Capybara. Don't freak out, but they're the largest rodent in the world."

"You mean those things are giant rats?" Wanda said.

"Remember, everything is a lot bigger here in the Amazon. But no, they're more like giant guinea pigs."

"My God, they're—"

The foliage suddenly shook around them and the ground trembled.

Frank yelled, "Get against the trees!"

He grabbed Dillon and shoved Wanda and Ally toward a tree trunk. James and Kathy dove for cover while Macky and Ezno took shelter at the next tree.

From high above, bodies and objects plummeted down through the tree branches with thunderous crashes. Scores of melon-size seedpods struck the ground like cannonballs. Woolly monkeys toppled out of the trees, landing hard on the ground. The dazed animals—those not killed outright from the high fall—scampered into the underbrush. Panic-stricken macaws and parrots squawked and flew out of the trees.

Leaves and other loosened foliage continued to rain down.

The tremor lasted for fifteen seconds before it stopped.

"Everyone all right?" Frank asked as the hiking group stepped warily away from the protective tree trunks.

"My God, Frank," Wanda said. "Did we just have another earthquake?"

"Yeah, a major one."

11

Ryan hadn't realized he'd dozed off until Jackie nudged him on the arm to wake him up. He opened his eyes and saw they were descending on a strip of water no wider than a six-lane highway. He braced as the floatplane touched down. Miles lowered the flaps and throttled back on the engine, coasting the aircraft to the sandy shoreline.

Ben opened his door and stepped out onto the pontoon. Jackie passed up Ben's daypack to Miles, who handed it to Ben. Jackie got out next. Ryan grabbed her pack, and his as well, as he made his way out of the plane.

"You and Jackie go ahead, I'll be right there," Ben told Ryan.

Jackie had already walked the length of the pontoon and made the short jump onto the beach. Ryan kept his balance with the two daypacks and stepped lively, leaping onto the sand.

A large crowd of Indian men, women, and children stood on the sandy embankment. As they were an indigenous tribe, Ryan assumed the men would be wearing fig leafs, the women to be bare breasted, and the children running around naked but instead, the Matis were dressed in t-shirts and tank tops—some even sporting popular athletic logos—and shorts, and all of them were barefoot.

Some of the women were holding infants. The other women were fanning themselves with rags and small towels.

Ryan quickly learned why when a cloud of sand flies buzzed his face. He shifted the strap of one of the backpacks to his other hand so he could swat at the annoying insects.

"They're not so bad once we get closer to the village," Jackie said and took her bag from Ryan.

He looked back and saw Ben with his pack on his back, carrying two red five-gallon gasoline cans. Ben hopped down onto the sand and walked up to Ryan.

"Can I give you a hand with one of those?" Ryan asked.

"Sure, thanks." Ben handed Ryan a gas can.

"What are these for?"

"Gifts. Whenever visiting the Matis, it is customary to bring an offering."

"But aren't they primitive? What would they need gas for?"

"Their outboards. Ryan, primitive or not, it's not like the Matis have been untouched by the outside world."

Ben knew enough of the language that he could communicate with a few of the men. They seemed friendly and laughed along with Ben as if he was the funniest man alive. They accepted the gifts and relieved Ben and Ryan of the burden of lugging the heavy gasoline cans.

As they started the short walk to the village, Ben gave Ryan a quick history lesson about the Matis people.

"There are only a few Matis tribes left today. Most of them died when the loggers invaded their lands, decimating the rainforest and bringing diseases like hepatitis and yellow fever."

"Sounds a lot like what happened to our Native Americans," Ryan said.

"You get the picture. Anyway, I thought you might want to participate in some of their rituals."

"Yeah, that would be great."

"Matis are firm believers in the animals' spirits, their favorite being the jaguar. That's why some call them the jaguar people. Don't stare, but you'll see they have facial tattoos that look like whiskers."

Ryan glanced over at a man walking to his right and saw the thin lines etched on his cheek.

Ben continued by saying, "The men practice certain rituals to make them great hunters. I have to warn you, they won't be pleasant. Still think you're up to it?"

"Sure," Ryan replied, knowing it was too late to back out even if he wanted to.

**

The village was made up of a circle of ten large thatch-roof huts suspended about eight feet off the ground in the event floodwaters were to overflow the riverbanks during the rainy season. In the center was the longhouse, the focal place for gatherings and conducting ceremonies, and where everyone ate.

Ben had arranged for Ryan to participate in the Ceremony of Mariwin, a ritual where men who looked like shamans with red masks and black-painted bodies went around the longhouse filled with people and whipped the women and children. Even though the children would run out crying, the lashings were never spiteful.

The men also participated in the ritual but did so outside and were generally flogged by other hunters. Ryan had already taken off his shirt and was standing in front of a five-foot post, his hands resting on the top.

Ben explained the purpose of the ritual was to transfer the energy of the spirits into the recipient's body.

The man standing behind Ryan had three four-foot long reeds in his left hand. He grabbed a single reed in his right hand and whipped Ryan across the back. The end of the switch wrapped around to sting Ryan's stomach and left a bright red welt on his fair skin.

Ryan winced but kept a brave face.

The flogger dropped the switch he had just used, selected a second one, and struck Ryan again. This time it stung even more and he had to grit his teeth.

Dropping the lash on the ground, the man administering pain took the last reed and slapped it across Ryan's back, this time leaving a third slash across his belly.

"So, how do you feel?" Ben asked, standing beside the onlookers, who were all grinning, some even laughing out loud.

"Like my stomach's one big paper cut." Ryan knew it'd be a while before he could put his shirt back on.

"Well, you got off easy. Now it's my turn." Ben removed his shirt but instead of stepping up to the post, he walked over to the longhouse where an elderly woman was waiting.

Jackie joined Ryan, and together they walked over to watch along with the other villagers.

"What's this ritual called?" Ryan asked.

"It's the Poison Frog Ceremony," Jackie replied. "From what I've heard, it's pretty brutal."

Ben stood in front of the woman, who was holding a burning stick. She placed the smoldering end onto Ben's flesh a few inches below his right nipple.

"That must hurt like hell," Ryan whispered to Jackie.

"That's not the half of it, just wait."

The hot ember left a charred piece of flesh in its wake, which the woman picked away with her fingernails. Ben's face tightened as he took in a deep breath.

The woman took another tiny stick and dabbed the tip into a substance smeared on a piece of bark that she was holding in her other hand. She took the end and held it on Ben's wound for a moment, then removed the applicator.

One of the men motioned for Ben to sit down on a cut piece of tree stump, which he did.

In a few short minutes, Ben began to sweat and grew pale.

"That's the frog poison taking over his body," Jackie said.

"Won't that kill him?" Ryan asked, finding it hard to believe she could be so calm when her friend had just been purposely poisoned. Shouldn't they be calling someone?

Ben looked deathly ill. He dropped to his hands and knees and vomited forcefully onto the dirt. Ryan thought it was humanly impossible to be able to heave that much puke. It was like watching Linda Blair auditioning for *The Exorcist.*

Ben struggled to his feet and looked over at Ryan and Jackie. "You guys will have to excuse me, but I'm going to have the shits." He stumbled across the clearing and headed for the nearest bushes and disappeared into the jungle.

The villagers were smiling and laughing. Watching Ben suffer the way he did seemed like a cruel hazing to Ryan. There was no telling how many times the Matis men indulged in their rituals, enduring pain and anguish in hopes of becoming better providers for their families.

It wasn't long before Ben finally came back. He looked much better and the color was back in his face. He looked at Ryan and smiled. "Can't say that was much fun but once it's all over, it gives you one hell of a high. You should give it a try."

"That's okay, Ben," Ryan said. "I think I'll give this one a pass."

12

Once back at the resort, everyone congregated in the lodge's small lobby to get the current news on the earthquake. Frank and Wanda stood at the counter conferring with Ignacio, while Ally and Dillon sat on a rattan settee across from Macky, James and Kathy, who were scrolling through their cell phones for the latest updates.

Ally had left her phone in her room to charge. Lately she'd had to charge it everyday and feared the battery needed replacing.

"Manaus was hit pretty bad," James said, reading from his phone. "They're estimating a magnitude of six point five."

"Here's some pictures," Kathy said.

Ally got up and stepped around the coffee table. She sat next to Kathy so she could get a good look at the small screen on Kathy's phone.

"Oh my," Ally said as Kathy flipped through the images: a hillside of collapsed stilt houses piled near the waterfront; a colonial church in ruin; beached and capsized boats in the marina; cars buried under rubble; ash-covered people running down the streets; a frightened woman holding her baby, their faces covered in blood.

Wanda was viewing her phone as well, checking her messages. "Here's a text from Ryan."

"Does he know anything about the quake?" Frank asked.

"I'm not sure. All he says is they arrived at the village."

"That's it?"

"Yeah. You want to see where they are?"

"Don't tell me you have tracking apps on your kids," Frank said.

"Not so loud or Ally might hear. Hey, what kind of a mother would I be if I didn't know where my children were 24/7?"

"I guess you have a point." Frank looked down at Wanda's phone. He saw a tiny red dot in a large mass of green. "Not many street addresses in the middle of the Amazon."

"I know, but it does give his GPS location."

Ignacio had stepped into the back office for moment but now was back. "I just watched a report. There's been much damage to the city. They've even had to close the airport. Which means we will not be getting any more guests, I am afraid to say."

"Also means we're stranded here until it reopens," Wanda said.

"It's not that bad, is it?" Frank said. "Remember, we're still on our honeymoon."

"I know, but it's going to be hard enjoying ourselves, knowing there are people out there suffering."

13

Ryan, Ben, and Jackie watched as a Matis hunter showed them how to fabricate a blow dart out of a thin stick. Near the center he formed a cottony-looking ball that would enable the dart to be propelled with a single puff of air once placed in the long tube. Each dart was tipped with curate, which poisoned only the blood and did not contaminate the eatable meat of the kill.

The blowgun was twelve feet in length and looked too cumbersome to be effective, not to mention the strength required to hold it out straight seemed impractical.

But when Ryan was handed a blowgun, he found it lighter than first believed, though he knew it would take considerable practice to master.

Ryan was definitely impressed when one of the Indians demonstrated the accuracy of his blowgun by hitting his intended target—a circle the size of a silver dollar coin carved on a post—from twenty yards away.

As the hunters started to band together in preparation for a hunt, Ryan thought it would be a good opportunity to talk with Jackie as Ben was conversing with a couple of the villagers.

"What do they usually hunt?" Ryan asked. At home, he liked to go fishing for steelhead and rainbow trout but never had reason to hunt. Sneaking up to kill an unsuspecting, defenseless creature just minding its own business in its natural habitat just seemed wrong—evenly cowardly.

For some unexplainable reason, catching a fish with a sharp barbed hook and watching it thrash around on the shore as it slowly suffocated to death never seemed to really bother him. If it were a mortally wounded deer lying on the ground and he had to watch the animal die—well, that would be inhumane. What was he doing going out on this hunt?

"Peccary," Jackie said.

"They're pigs, right?"

"Sort of."

Ever since they had arrived at the village, Ryan had a burning question he wanted to ask Jackie, her being the zoologist major.

"I've been noticing a lot of monkeys playing with the kids and hanging around the village for scraps. Don't they ever worry about disease, keeping them as pets?"

Jackie gave Ryan a strange look. She placed her hand on his arm and was about to say something, when Ben called out, "Come on, you two, we're leaving."

Six hunters took the lead and walked along separate paths, stopping every so often to gaze up into the trees. One of the men carried two blowguns, one of which was for either Ben or Ryan's use. Ryan hoped when it came time for him to bow out, he could do it in way so as not to offend the tribesmen.

That time came all too soon.

One of the hunters was pointing up into a tall tree.

Ryan looked up but he wasn't sure what the man was showing the others; it was so dark up in the tightly clustered leaves.

The man carrying the two blowguns came up to Ryan. He placed the weapons on the ground, picked one up, and inserted a dart. He handed the blowgun to Ryan and pointed up at the tree.

Again, Ryan stared up. "I'm sorry, but I don't think I can do this."

"Ryan, just give it a go," Ben said.

"I don't know what he wants me to shoot."

"Just do it," Ben said firmly.

Ryan saw a shape moving in the dark shadows. He could hear birds high up in the branches, squawking and fluttering their wings. He raised the long blowgun, tilted his head back, and blew as hard as he could.

A second later, something fell through the branches.

"Talk about a lucky shot," Ben said, clapping Ryan on the back.

Ryan stepped back as a small body hit the ground.

"It's a spider monkey," Jackie said.

Lying there in the dirt, it looked human-like with its gangly arms and legs and long tail. Its fur was so black Ryan hadn't noticed the other creature attached until Jackie said, "And it has a baby."

Ryan put the blowgun down, feeling sick to his stomach by what he had just done.

One of the Indians squatted next to the dead monkey and pulled off the infant still clutching on to its mother's fur. He took a poison dart and stuck the tip into the baby, killing it instantly.

"My God, why'd he do that?" Ryan said, totally shocked.

"It was still nursing and too young to survive without its mother and would have died anyway," Jackie explained.

"Did he really have to kill it?"

"You have to understand, Ryan, this is how these people live," Ben said.

Ryan felt so ashamed. Not only had he killed the mother, he was also responsible for the infant having to be put down. He felt like a monster and knew if his sister and his little brother were here, they too would be sickened by what he had done.

"I guess I'm confused," Ryan said. "What about those monkeys back at the village?"

"A lot of the time when they kill a monkey, it's a female with a youngster," Jackie said. "If it can fend for itself, the hunter will bring it back to the village."

"To keep as a pet? That seems a little cold," Ryan said, unable to mask the disgust in his voice.

"No, Ryan," Jackie said. "Because monkey is their staple diet."

14

After returning from the hunt, Ryan had walked off to spend some time alone, as he was still upset about unintentionally killing the mother monkey and even more distraught about her infant's fate.

It wasn't long before Jackie tracked him down.

"There you are," she said. "Thought I'd lost you."

"No, I'm right here."

"I'm sorry about what happened out there. Life in the Amazon can be pretty harsh."

"You're telling me. How do you cope with it?"

Jackie let out a little laugh. "Believe me, there're things I've seen that have brought me to tears."

"Like what?"

"I don't think you really want to know."

"Yeah, you're probably right," Ryan said. "Talk about a culture shock."

"Back home we're spoiled," Jackie said. "You want anything; you just go to the supermarket. Everything is neat and nicely packaged and no one has to get their hands dirty. Out here, these people have to hunt, harvest their own crops, and survive in the jungle."

"I'm not being judgmental."

"I know you're not. It's a just big contrast from what we're used to."

"I hope I haven't let you guys down."

"Ryan, if you had acted any different, I would have been disappointed."

"Well, I'll try and keep it together."

"Anyway, they wanted me to fetch you as some of the villagers are going down to the river to do some fishing."

"Then we better not keep them waiting."

By the time Ryan and Jackie got to the shore, there was a small congregation of women standing at the mouth of a cove about as large as a backyard swimming pool.

Each woman was carrying a cloth sack. They spread out along the perimeter of the murky body of water.

"I don't see anyone with a fishing pole, or a net," Ryan said.

"That's because here they don't need them," Jackie replied.

Ryan watched as the women lobbed their sacks into the water.

"Why'd they do that?"

"Wait and you'll see."

A single fish rose to the surface, then another, and more still, until there were over a hundred fish floating on their sides. The women waded into the shallow water and began scooping up the fish.

"Did they just poison the water?" Ryan asked, astonished they would go to such an extreme instead of a more traditional method.

"Not exactly. It's the affects of the huaca plant. That's what was in those sacks the women were throwing. It depletes the oxygen in the water."

"Like tossing in a stick of dynamite."

"The same effect."

It was dusk when they returned to the village. Ben and a few other men were standing around a large fire pit with a built-up grate. The flames were heavily stoked, licking almost three feet high up through the metal slats.

Ryan couldn't quite make out what they were cooking. He felt Jackie tug at his arm.

"I don't think you want to go over there."

"That bad, eh?"

"After what you've seen today, yes. I have an idea. Let's sneak away and go check on Miles."

"The pilot? I thought he left."

"No, he's tied up a little ways downstream. I'm sure he'd be happy to see us."

"Lead the way."

Ben and the villagers were already gathering in the longhouse for their evening feast. Doing their best so as not to be seen, Ryan and Jackie snuck into a hut and retrieved their daypacks. They waited until they were far enough away before turning on their flashlights. Jackie took the lead as they headed down a sandy path.

The moon was almost full, casting a shimmer over the tranquil river.

After rounding a bend, Ryan spotted the pilot's campfire and the floatplane moored up to the shore.

"Mind if we join you?" Jackie asked, walking into the camp.

Miles looked up and gave the young woman a smile. "Well, hi there. Wasn't expecting visitors."

"Thought you might like the company," Jackie said, taking a seat by the fire.

"How come you didn't come into the village?" Ryan asked. He sat down on the sand next to Jackie.

"It's better I don't," Miles said. His face was sweaty and he looked a little tired as he picked up a whisky bottle and offered it to Jackie.

"Thanks." Jackie twisted off the cap and, like the hard-drinking love interest of Indiana Jones, Marion Ravenwood, she took a long pull on the bottle. She blew out a breath and handed the bottle to Ryan, who was duly impressed.

He raised the bottle and took a swig. The whisky burned down his gullet like Drano cleaning out a drainpipe. He tried not to show a reaction but coughed anyway.

Miles threw another piece of wood on the fire.

They passed the bottle around for the best part of an hour. Ryan was already feeling a buzz. He was surprised Jackie could hold her liquor so well; or would it catch up to her later? Ryan listened while Jackie shared a couple stories of her experiences in the jungle. Miles also had a few tales.

Not wanting to overstay their welcome—and gluttonously polish off the rest of Miles' whiskey—Jackie suggested they should get back to the village.

Once Ryan and Jackie were out of earshot, Ryan said, "Did he seem all right to you?"

"What d'you mean?" Jackie slurred.

"I don't know. He didn't look well."

"He was probably just a little drunk."

Ryan caught Jackie as she stumbled.

"Whoa, are *you* okay?"

"Be a pal and hold back my hair."

"What?" Ryan caught on pretty quick when Jackie bent over and hurled on her boots. He did his best to keep her hair out of her face as she vomited a second time. In a strange way, it made him feel better about himself knowing she wasn't so tough after all.

15

Ryan was more than glad to be leaving. Rather than have Miles taxi the floatplane up to the beach by the village, Jackie convinced Ben they should just go down to where Miles had camped for the night.

Jackie and Ryan had headed out first, Ben not so far behind. As he was taller than the Indians accompanying him, it gave him an air of authority, as if he were their warrior chief. At least that is how Ryan interpreted the sight every time he looked over his shoulder.

It was early light when they arrived where Miles had camped out. He had already packed up his things and had taken the time to rake over the fire pit, restoring the spot just the way he had found it.

The pilot was sitting in the cockpit, consulting his notebook and going through his system check-off list.

"Morning," Jackie said, climbing through the open passenger door.

Miles grunted a reply and kept gazing down at the binder.

Ryan handed the two daypacks up and Jackie carried them to the back of the plane and stored them behind the rear seats. They both sat in the same seats they had occupied in the previous flight. Looking out the side window, Ryan could see Ben bidding the villagers a farewell like a missionary promising to return with hope for a better life. The goodbyes stretched on for minutes.

"Come on, Ben!" Jackie called out.

Ben eventually disengaged himself from the villagers crowded around him and backed up toward the plane, all the time waving.

"He can be so pompous at times," Jackie said in a low voice so only Ryan could hear.

"Sounds like someone got up on the wrong side of the hammock."

"Not funny."

Ben lobbed his rucksack into the cockpit, pulled himself up onto the copilot's seat, and closed the door.

Everyone put on their headsets as Miles primed the oil pump and checked his gauges. He started up the engine and the propeller whirled outside the windshield. Even with the headphones, the noise was loud.

Miles steered the floatplane out into the middle of the river and throttled the engine. The aircraft continued to gain speed until it finally left the water and soared up over the treetops.

Ryan looked back out the window expecting to see the Matis village, but the plane had already banked over the misty rainforest canopy. Now there was nothing else to do but sit back and relax. He was looking forward to getting back to the resort. Having a shower, and getting some food, especially since he had skipped the meal served at the longhouse. As he hadn't slept well the previous night, he decided to grab twenty winks and closed his eyes.

He was in a deep slumber when Jackie shook his arm.

"What..."

"Jesus, Ben, do something!" she yelled.

"I don't know how to fly this thing," he screamed back.

Ryan opened his eyes and sat up in his seat. "What's going on?"

"Miles just had a heart attack."

Ryan unbuckled his seatbelt so he could get a good look at the pilot. Miles was slumped forward with his eyes closed and his chin on his chest. "We need to try giving him CPR."

Ben started to reach over and unbuckle Miles but when he did, he bumped the yoke and the plane's nose started to dip.

"Pull it back, pull it back," Jackie screamed.

Ben grabbed the stick and drew the yoke back into position.

"Jackie and I'll try to revive Miles," Ryan said, surprised he was the one taking control of the situation instead of the two older college students.

Ryan reached around and released Miles' seatbelt. He grabbed the man around the chest and hoisted him out of the seat. Ryan stepped back and pulled Miles down on the floor between the passenger seats. He unzipped the pilot's bomber jacket, placed one hand over the other palm down on the center of the man's chest and immediately started chest compressions like he had learned during a special session in his physical education class when he was a junior back in high school.

Once he had counted off thirty chest compressions, he sat upright and nodded for Jackie to perform mouth-to-mouth resuscitation.

Jackie checked to make sure Mile's airway was clear and he hadn't swallowed his tongue. She tilted his head back and pinched his nose then leaned down and blew two quick puffs of air into his mouth. Sitting back, she gave Ryan room so he could lean over and continue the compressions.

They kept up the medical emergency, alternating back and forth.

"Maybe we can reach someone on the radio," Ben said. He placed his hand on the console and fiddled with a dial. "Mayday, mayday, this is the..." he stopped and looked around the cockpit. "Hell, I don't even know our call sign."

"Just tell them its Miles Gifford's plane," Ryan said, pumping on Miles' chest.

"Wait a minute," Ben said, tapping the side of his headset. "Is this thing even working?"

Jackie turned and sniffed. "I smell smoke."

Ryan could smell it, too. It was coming from the console. He took off his headset and could hear a crackling sound. And then he saw sparks. He looked down by his feet and saw a fire extinguisher clamped to the bulkhead. He stopped the compressions realizing there was no point reviving the pilot if the plane was on fire. Undoing the clamp, he grabbed the canister, pulled the pin, and blasted the dashboard with white fire retardant and put out the small fire.

"This is not good," Ben said, gazing at the foam-covered instrument panel. The electrical fire had fried the wiring, as all the needles on the gauges were no longer registering.

"Now I have no idea of our heading," Ben said.

"Or how much fuel we have," Ryan said. He looked down at the ashen-face pilot lying on the floor.

The plane lurched as the engine sputtered.

"Oh my God, we're going down," Jackie said.

Ryan pulled his cell phone out of his pocket to text his mom goodbye.

16

A map of the cities surrounding Manaus was spread out on the lobby table generally used for displaying brochures and small booklets with useful travel tips.

Frank was running his finger from one location to the next, reading off city names while James and Kathy consulted their cell phones to see how that particular city had withstood the devastating earthquake. Macky was having problems with his phone and went outside to see if he could get better reception.

"Looks like Caldeira was hit pretty hard as well," James said.

"We might have trouble getting out of here," Frank said.

Wanda was sitting on the settee next to Ally and Dillon. She'd taken her cell phone out of her jean pocket as it was bulky and placed it on the coffee table.

"Do you think Ryan's all right?" Ally asked.

"The way Frank explained it, Ryan's a good ways away. He probably doesn't even know what's happening here. Just as well. I wouldn't want him to worry about us and spoil his trip."

"Are we going to sit here all day?" Dillon whined, already bored.

"I know it's hard for you to understand, but this is very serious. We might be stuck here for some time."

"Then let's go do something."

"Not right yet. You're going to have to be a little patient."

Kathy had just finished looking at another city and glanced up at Frank, shaking her head.

"Not looking good," Frank said to Wanda.

Wanda's phone *binged*, signaling she had an incoming text message.

She reached over, picked up her phone, and checked her email.

"Oh my God," she said, once she'd read the text.

"What is it?" Frank said, turning away from the table and looking over at his wife.

"Miles Gifford had a heart attack."

"Is he okay?" Frank asked.

Wanda glanced back down at her phone for a second then looked up with a horrified look on her face. "He's dead."

"Oh, no. That means they're stranded at that village."

"Frank, you don't understand. They've already left.

"What?"

"They're flying without a pilot."

17

Ryan had been on plenty of wild amusement rides before but never anything as scary as being trapped in an airplane 10,000 feet in the sky without a pilot and not knowing when the fuel would run out, especially when the engine had sputtered and they thought they were going to crash. Fortunately, he had been paying attention watching Miles fiddling with the mixture levers before each flight and was able to make similar adjustments and get the engine running somewhat steady.

Out of respect, Ryan had taken Miles' flight jacket off and draped it over the dead man's head and upper body. Jackie had been especially shaken up and was back in her seat. Her eyes were red from crying.

Even though Ben professed he couldn't fly the aircraft, he seemed to be doing a fair enough job of it, as they hadn't crashed yet. Basically, he had been keeping the yoke steady and letting the plane pretty much fly itself.

They had their headsets back on so they could talk to one another.

"How long have we been in the air?" Ryan asked, not sure how long he had been napping before being awaken by Jackie.

"Three hours, maybe," Ben replied.

Ryan had been glancing out the window on occasion, hoping to see a village or a small town, any sign of civilization, but each time there was only a massive expanse of green. But now he could see a river below with same branching tributaries that looked like tiny veins splitting away from a large artery.

Ben yelled and began drumming his feet down on the cockpit floor.

"What wrong?"

"They're coming out of the instrument panel!"

Jackie moved forward in her seat. "Oh my God."

Ryan saw thousands of black specks racing out of every hole and crack in the instrument panel. Some were falling out from the bottom of the housing like ground pepper sifting out of a grinder. "What are they?"

"Crazy ants," Jackie said, already slapping a pant leg.

"Seriously, they're called crazy ants?"

"Don't let too many of them get on you," Jackie warned, grabbing an old copy of *Aviation History* tucked in the pocket behind the pilot's seat. She rolled up the magazine and began swatting at the pesky insects before they could bite her.

Ryan was getting the idea how the insects got their name. The ants were scrambling crazily in every direction like they had just blundered onto a sizzling hot plate.

"They're probably what started the fire," Ben shouted, using his free hand to slap at his attackers.

"You're saying the ants started the fire," Ryan said disbelievingly but gave him the idea to grab the extinguisher for the second time. He sprayed the cockpit floor, smothering the frantic swarm.

"They eat through the electrical and cause short circuits," Jackie yelled. "Probably crawled aboard while Miles was camped on the shore."

"And that's not all," Ben said and looked over his shoulder. "They foul up the fuel line."

And then, as if on cue, the engine quit.

The floatplane continued to glide, but they were losing altitude. Ryan got the same sensation in his stomach he'd get whenever he was in a descending elevator.

The nose of the plane dipped and Ben pulled back on the yoke, which had no effect leveling the aircraft. Instead, the floatplane banked to the right, throwing Jackie up against Ryan and pinning him against the window.

"Get your seatbelt on," Ryan told Jackie.

Jackie moved back to her seat and strapped herself in. Ryan fastened his seatbelt.

The ants were no longer a threat as they struggled in the thick foam covering most of the floor of the cockpit and parts of the passenger area.

Ryan looked out the windshield.

They were going down fast.

Directly in their path was a long, thin body of water. "Ben, we still have a chance. Shoot for the river."

It was plain to see Ben had no real control of the plane. If they landed on the water, it would be a miracle.

But as they banked over the trees, Ryan saw what he thought at first to be calm waters was actually a fast flowing river. The rapids ran farther downriver to a massive jumble of rocks and a waterfall.

"Brace yourselves!" Ben yelled.

Ryan and Jackie bent forward and laced their fingers behind their heads.

The impact was so great the bolts on Ryan's seat snapped off and he was thrown up against the upright of the copilot's seat. He glanced over his shoulder at Jackie, who must have hit her head on the bulkhead. There was blood trickling down the side of her face from a cut on her forehead.

The floatplane took another bounce and came down with a loud screech. Ryan looked out the window and caught a glimpse of one of the pontoons behind, mangled on some boulders.

Hitting the water again and missing a pontoon, the plane's wing dipped down into the water.

Ben unbuckled his seatbelt and kicked open the passenger door. A forceful gush of water rushed into the cockpit.

"Grab your bags," he yelled, snatching his rucksack and bailing out the door.

"Jackie, come on," Ryan said, getting out of his seat.

"I can't. My buckle won't open."

Ryan reached down and tried to unsnap the seatbelt but it was jammed.

The water was already up to Jackie's knees.

"Ryan, do something."

He reached in his front jean pocket and took out his folded knife. He opened the blade and began sawing at the strap. It was taking longer than he thought. He couldn't remember the last time he'd sharpened his knife.

The water level was up to Jackie's stomach, and rising fast, so he could no longer see what he was doing, or the progress he was making, cutting through the constraint.

The strap finally severed and Ryan pulled Jackie out of her seat. He guided her to the door opening and had to brace himself as he pushed her out against the incoming flood of water. He wanted to go back and retrieve their daypacks but he knew if he tried he'd drown for sure.

He took a big gulp of air, and propelled himself out of the cockpit. He swam underwater, just missing the wing as the submerging airplane was dragged downstream by the strong current.

Breaking the surface, Ryan turned around in the rapids to get his bearings but his only choice was to swim for the nearest shore. By the time he reached the bank, he was totally exhausted and clawed up the muddy embankment on his belly.

Taking a few deep breaths, he turned over, and managed to sit up.

He looked upstream but didn't see any sign of Ben or Jackie. He gazed across the river and scanned the opposite shore but saw no one. He turned to look downstream but he was at a crook in the river and couldn't see beyond the tight cluster of trees.

Jackie and Ben were nowhere to be seen; his biggest fear they had both drowned.

Which meant he was now alone—lost in the jungle.

His chances of being rescued were as slim as finding a penny in a copper mine.

18

Wanda stared impatiently at her phone. "Come on, Ryan. Answer me back."

"Try him again," Ally said.

"I've already sent him three texts."

Frank was still standing at the table. He looked up from the map. "You can't call him?"

"No," Wanda said. "For some reason text is the only thing that works out here."

"Bring your phone over here," Frank said.

Wanda got up from the settee and joined Frank at the table.

"Show me that app again," Frank whispered. "Maybe I can pinpoint his location on this map."

Wanda swiped her finger across the glass face of her phone, tapped on a small multi-colored square and another screen popped up with a zoomed in map of the lower region of Brazil.

"Can you zoom out a bit?" Frank asked.

"Sure." Wanda tapped on the screen and the lettering and the dots identifying the cities shrunk so as to display more of the surrounding area.

"I take those two red markers are Ally and Dillon, here at the resort."

"That's right."

"I don't see Ryan. Zoom out some more."

Wanda flicked the screen.

"There he is," Frank said, spotting Ryan's positioning marker. "Watch and see if it changes."

They stared at the screen for almost five minutes but the marker stayed in the same position.

"Hmm," Frank murmured.

"What?"

"It's not moving. I think the plane crashed."

"Oh my God," Wanda said, leaning on the table, trying not to show emotion and alarm Ally and Dillon.

James and Kathy had stepped out to stretch their legs and check up on Macky.

Frank consulted the cell phone one more time before looking back at the map. He ran his finger across the paper. "I believe he's somewhere...," he said, then stabbed the map with his finger, "Here!"

"Thank God. So you know where he is," Wanda said.

"Well, not exactly. That's sort of no man's land. I don't think anyone's ever been in that region of the jungle before. At least, no one I know of."

"What you're telling me is it's unexplored."

"That's right. You have to realize there's over two billion square miles of rainforest out there."

"So what do we do?"

"Now we know where he is, we can call and mount an air search. I'm sure Miles's plane has a distress beacon. Shouldn't be too difficult to find."

"Mom, Dillon's being a pill," Ally said, startling Frank and Wanda when she suddenly appeared at the table. She glanced down and saw the image on Wanda's phone. "What's that?"

Wanda placed her hand over the screen. "Nothing."

"You have one of those kid trackers on your phone," Ally said accusingly.

"And it's a good thing I do."

"I can't believe you've been spying on us." Ally turned, walked over, and plopped down on the settee next to Dillon, glowering.

Wanda glared at her daughter. "Boy, sometimes..."

"It's okay," Frank said, putting his arm around Wanda's shoulder to calm her down. "You two can sort that out later. Right now, we have to make some phone calls. Don't worry, the authorities will find him."

19

Ryan stood on the bank and yelled out Jackie's name a number of times. When he didn't get a reply, he called for Ben, but still no answer from either one of them. He kept swatting away gnats; they wouldn't leave him alone. The tiny pests were in his ears, flying up his nostrils, and doing everything in their power to make him as miserable as possible.

A couple mosquitoes joined in but Ryan squashed them when they landed on his mud-caked arm. That's when he realized the only part of him not covered in mud was his face. He bent down and scooped up a handful of mud and smeared it all over his face and the back of his neck, even in and around his ears.

Soon the gnats lost interest and went on their merry way. Though it hadn't been intentional, Ryan had discovered the perfect insect deterrent, which was lucky for him as he didn't have bug repellent. The only things he possessed at the moment were the clothes on his back, his pocketknife, and a cell phone he doubted was much good as it had been submerged in water and was probably a goner. He checked the phone anyway and confirmed his suspicion as the glass face was fogged up and the device wouldn't respond.

He glanced around to assess his situation, which couldn't have been any bleaker if he had been stranded on the moon. He couldn't see farther downstream because of the bend in the river. The shoreline across the river was made up of a vast system of tree roots, strangler vines, and no proper beaches. The tightly clustered trees towered over one hundred feet over the water and the vegetation was so thick the face of the jungle looked like one giant, green wall.

Ryan turned and looked inland. The rainforest on his side looked just as inaccessible. He knew it would be wiser to follow the river rather than to venture into the jungle, but he knew the thickness of the vegetation made that impossible on foot. He thought about trying to swim downstream, but that seemed too dangerous. Maybe he could float on a log, but he didn't see anything that might keep him afloat. Or he could spend eternity cutting down a tree with his pocketknife, whittling out a hull, and eventually canoe down.

No matter what option he chose, as ridiculous as they all were, the idea of going down the rapids was pure ludicrous as he would just end up dying going over the falls.

Ryan cupped his hands around his mouth and yelled, "Jackie! Can you hear me?"

The only thing he heard was the drone of the katydids along with birdcalls and an eerie screeching somewhere in the trees around the bend.

That's when Ryan realized it was Jackie, screaming for her life.

20

The lobby sounded like a customer service call center with everyone speaking loudly into their phones as James, Kathy, and Macky had returned and were pitching in to launch a rescue effort.

James put down his phone in disgust. "I was on hold for twenty minutes and no one ever came back to me."

Kathy finally gave up. "I can't get through."

"The lines are all tied up," Ignacio said.

"My phone's useless," Macky confessed.

"It's a national emergency," Frank said. "I doubt very seriously if we will be able to get anyone to help us."

"What are we going to do?" Wanda asked.

"I really don't know."

Ally got up from the settee and came over to her mother. "Mom, I'm sorry about earlier. I didn't mean to be a brat."

Wanda gave her daughter a smile. "We're all a little stressed right now. I wasn't being sneaky."

"I know. What kind of sheriff would you be if you didn't know where your own kids were?"

"I just worry about you guys."

"So what do we do now?"

"That's a good question."

"Could you make it by boat?" Ignacio asked Frank.

"Well, let me see," Frank said, and spent a moment using his finger to trace a route from the resort to where he thought Ryan might be. "Yes, I believe so, but where are we going to get a boat?"

"We have one here."

"All I've seen are canoes," Frank said.

"No, we have a proper boat back in the cove," Ignacio said. "We sometimes use it to take guests back to the city. I can take you to find your son."

"But that might take days."

"Our boat is fast and well equipped. We have lights to run at night."

Frank looked at Wanda. "This could be our only chance."

"Then we should go."

"We?"

"I'm going, too."

"It's a lot different out there in the jungle than it is here at the resort."

"I'm still going," Wanda said stubbornly.

"It's too dangerous."

"Frank, I'm a sheriff, for crying out loud."

"Don't say I didn't warn you."

"Duly noted."

"We're going as well," James said.

"Oh, I don't know if—"

"Remember our friends are out there, too," Kathy said after interrupting Frank.

Frank turned to Ignacio. "Is there enough room for all of us?"

"There is," Ignacio said. "But no more."

"What about Dillon and me?" Ally said.

"I'll need you both to stay here," Wanda said.

"But Mom—"

"Well, if you have a full crew, looks like I'm also staying," Macky said then looked at Ally. "That is, if you don't mind the company?"

"Thanks, Macky."

"Then I suggest everyone grab what you need," Frank said. "We're leaving in an hour."

21

Ryan fought his way through the dense foliage wishing he had a machete or a hatchet, anything that would cut through the entanglement instead of only a silly pocketknife. He pushed through the heavy vegetation, tripping over roots and vines, until he came out of the trees on the other side of the bend.

He cupped his hand around his mouth and yelled, "Jackie! Where are you?"

That's when he heard Jackie shout, "I'm over here. Hurry!"

Ryan looked over in the direction he had heard her voice, but he couldn't see her. All he saw was the torrential river and a catchall cove with driftwood and debris stacked high in the water.

As he approached the water's edge, a hand shot up from under a leafy branch. "I'm down here!"

Wading into the water, Ryan cut a path through the flotsam until he reached Jackie, who was pinned under a large bough, her face barely above water.

"Hold on, I'm going to get you out," Ryan shouted over the roar of the turbulent rapids. He started yanking off smaller branches to clear room so he could lift the thick timber that was holding Jackie down. On dry land, it would have been impossible for him to get it off the ground, but half-floating in the water, he knew he had a chance of moving it enough so Jackie could slip free.

"When I say *when*, I want you to slide toward me," Ryan said, looking down at Jackie's face. "Got it?"

"Got it," Jackie said, gulping in a mouthful of water and spitting it out.

Ryan wrapped his arms around the bough and bent his knees. "When!" He stood and raised the heavy tree branch. Jackie ducked her head under the water and pushed her body toward Ryan. As soon as she was clear, Ryan dropped the bough before straining his back.

He grabbed her by the hands and pulled her up out of the water onto her feet. "Are you okay?"

"I thought for sure I was going to die..." And then she collapsed into him.

Ryan held her in his arms.

"Don't worry, I've got you."

22

Ignacio and Enzo had already prepared the boat with enough supplies to last a week. Ten five-gallon gasoline cans had been brought on board as added fuel for the long voyage and were strapped down at the stern in front of the two 65-horsepower Chrysler outboard engines mounted on the transom. A permanent three-foot wide rubber bumper wrapped all the way around the vessel's hull, which had a flat bottom for navigating shallow waters.

It was almost twilight when Frank and Wanda came down the pier, carrying their bags. The sun behind them was setting behind the trees on the opposite bank, casting a pink hue over the river.

Wanda handed Frank her bag and climbed aboard the rescue boat. Frank tossed both bags up on the narrow deck, which ran around a pilothouse. He stepped up and opened the rear door.

Ignacio sat at the helm and was checking to make sure everything operated correctly. He threw some toggle switches, one after the other. The outside spotlights and floodlights came on briefly then turned off.

Frank and Wanda stepped inside. There were bench seats on either side with room underneath so they could stow their bags.

"Do you have any firearms onboard?" Wanda asked.

Ignacio turned around in his seat. "Yes, we do." He pounded on the window to get Enzo's attention, who was standing outside at the bull-nosed bow next to the mooring cleat.

Enzo hurried down the side of the pilothouse and came in.

Ignacio pointed at a long locker against the bulkhead.

Digging in his pocket, Enzo pulled out a small ring of keys. He went over to the footlocker, found the corresponding key, and opened the padlock. He lifted the lid back.

"Well, I wasn't expecting all that," Frank said, staring down at the assortment of guns and the well-stocked boxes of ammunition. He turned to Ignacio. "Were you expecting trouble?"

"Always."

Wanda reached in and pulled out a holster with a nine-millimeter pistol. "It's a Browning, just like my service weapon."

"That's actually mine, but you can use it if you like," Ignacio said.

"Well, thank you." Wanda coiled the belt and laid the holster on the bench seat where she would be sitting.

Frank lifted one of the short barrel shotguns out of the locker. It was a good bush gun for short range. He opened the breech and stared down the twin tubes. He snapped it closed and laid it back in the box next to three other shotguns lying in precut foam along with a couple of hunting rifles with scopes. There were three small caliber revolvers in a small box without a lid, an assortment of different length knives in sheaths, and half a dozen machetes with looped lanyards for slipping over the wrist.

James and Kathy ran down the pier and scampered aboard the boat.

"Sorry," Kathy apologized as she rushed in and sat down. James shoved his bag under the seat. He glanced over and saw the weapons in the footlocker. "That's quite the arsenal."

"I'm not really much of a gun person," Kathy said.

"That's perfectly okay," Wanda said. She nodded to Enzo and he closed the lid of the weapons locker and replaced the padlock.

"We're ready to go," Ignacio said. He started the electrical ignition and the two powerful outboards roared. Enzo went on deck and cast off the mooring lines forward and aft.

The rescue boat pulled away from the pier.

Frank and Wanda stepped out of the pilothouse and stood on the stern.

Ally, Dillon, Macky, and Murilo had gathered on the beach and were yelling goodbye and waving. Frank and Wanda waved back.

The lights came on and the boat started to pick up speed.

Wanda kept waving even though she could no longer see Ally and Dillon.

"We better go in before we fall overboard," Frank said and they went inside.

23

Ryan and Jackie's voices were getting hoarse from yelling so they finally gave up.

"It's no use," Ryan said. "He's not hearing us."

"You don't think he got swept over the falls?"

"I don't know."

Raindrops started coming down.

Ryan looked up at the battleship-gray clouds. "Oh, isn't this great. As if we're not wet enough, now it has to rain."

And then the deluge unleashed. So heavy, Ryan and Jackie dashed for the trees to seek shelter.

"Oh my God," Jackie squealed. "It's coming down buckets!"

Running under the canopy, the rainstorm was even louder as the downpour pelted the rainforest. It smelled musty under the wet, glistening foliage. Nightfall was only minutes away as they stood in the shadowy gloom.

Jackie's light-colored blouse clung to her like a second skin. Ryan could see her black bra through the damp fabric.

"What's that?" he asked and pointed at her stomach area.

Jackie looked down and lifted up her blouse.

"It's a leech!"

Ryan unbuttoned his shirt and took it off.

"Oh Ryan, they're all over you."

They stripped out of their clothes, even out of their socks and boots.

"They're so disgusting," Jackie said. "You do me, I'll do you." She began plucking off the black slug-like parasites attached to Ryan's chest and abdomen while he worked on her stomach and shoulders, which after being removed left red, oval-shaped teeth marks. Jackie turned around so Ryan could work on her back and the backs of her legs. Once he was done, he turned and let Jackie remove the rest of the leeches still clinging to his flesh.

Ryan opened the waistband of his briefs and looked down and was thankful he didn't see any leeches.

Watching Ryan, Jackie turned around and checked herself.

"Wait," Ryan said. He reached over and removed a leech from her right butt cheek. "Okay, you're good."

"Well, that was fun," Jackie said, facing Ryan.

"More like a weird date."

Jackie let out a little laugh. "Better check your clothes good before putting them back on."

"I will," Ryan said but he couldn't stop grinning.

"Okay, you saw my junk, I saw yours."

Ryan burst out laughing. "I wouldn't exactly call it *junk*."

"Shut up." Jackie gave him a hip check as he was trying to step into his jeans. He hopped on one foot trying his best not to fall down.

Once they were fully dressed, Ryan reached in his pocket and took out his cell phone.

"Oh my God, you have your phone."

"Don't you?" Ryan asked.

"Like a stooge, I left it in my daypack."

"Well, I doubt if it even works."

"Sure, it should. Aren't they all waterproof?"

"Apparently, not this one." Ryan tried turning it on anyway. After waiting a few seconds, he was surprised to see the screen light up. "Well, I'll be."

They stared at the only source of light, as it was already dark. Ryan switched to the flashlight app.

"We need to find somewhere to hold up for the night," Jackie said. "Preferably off the ground."

"What, like in a tree?"

"That would be the safest place, yes."

Ryan could hear tiny creatures scuttling and slithering in the underbrush. "We better hurry up."

Holding his phone out in front of him, Ryan and Jackie traipsed through the wet jungle. They soon discovered an enormous tree, which appeared to be actually four trees that had grown together into one. One of the trunks sloped down and looked easy to scale.

Ryan held the cell phone light for Jackie so she could shimmy up.

"This is perfect," Jackie said, after she'd climbed up twenty feet. "It's roomy enough for us to sleep."

Ryan ascended the trunk to their hidey-hole, which was a hollow formed during the growth of the tightly grouped trees.

"Have you tried making a call?" Jackie asked, looking at Ryan's cell phone in his hand.

"I sent a text just before we crashed," Ryan said.

"To who?"

"My mom."

"What did she say?"

"I don't know. I haven't checked my messages."

"Oh my God, what are you waiting for? Maybe they're sending help."

Ryan looked down at the lit screen just as the image flickered and went black.

"Damn. There goes my battery."

24

Despite the recent torrential downpour, Ben was able to collect enough dry tinder and get a fire going. He'd found a good spot under a cover of elephant-ear fronds, which allowed the smoke to filter up through the trees but also deflected the heat and warmed him up.

He had laid out some of the contents of his rucksack: flashlight, a packet of trail mix, a first aid kit, and a pair of dry socks. He'd lost his cell phone as it had been in a side pouch that had been torn away. Not only had the waterproof daypack been essential in preventing his stuff from getting waterlogged, its buoyancy had saved his life. The moment he had exited the plane, he'd been swept downstream; clinging onto his bag like it was a life preserver.

It had been a constant struggle to keep his head up out of the water as the swift current carried him barreling down the choppy river. He'd used his pack to cushion each time he was plowed into a partially submerged boulder. He'd tried to grab on but the surfaces were always too slimy and his fingers would slip off.

He remembered the rising mist and the loud roar of the falls.

By some miracle, he had latched onto a piece of wood wedged between two rocks and he was finally able to pull himself up out of the water. Stepping onto the rocky beach, he'd glanced back and saw a distant cove on the opposite shore.

When the damaged floatplane had drifted by and plummeted over the falls, he wished there could have been something he could have done to save Jackie and Ryan.

Being the sole survivor didn't seem like much of a consolation, especially when he had to live with the thought his friends had gone to a watery grave.

There was no point on dwelling on that now. He had to attend to his scrapes and cuts. An open wound only invited trouble. The last thing he wanted was an egg-laying blowfly boring under his skin. Not to mention other parasites worming into his flesh and entering his blood stream. It was the smallest creatures that were the most dangerous in the Amazon. The malaria-carrying mosquito had killed more people than all the world wars combined.

Ben used a disinfectant and dabbed his abrasions. He used the tiny scissors in the emergency kit and cut small bandage swaths and taped them over each wound. After he had covered every injury, he put everything back in the plastic box.

He broke up some branches and fed the fire. The flame rose like a red-copper snake. He rubbed his hands together feeling the warmth.

He picked up the packet of trail mix and tore open the top. He popped a handful of the food into his mouth and savored the salty nuts and the chewy raisins.

Ben sat back against a tree trunk and watched the flames of the fire flickering in the middle of the surrounding darkness.

He could hear rustling all around him as nocturnal predators began their nightlong search for prey.

Sooner or later, he knew he would have to sleep.

25

They'd been traveling on the river for nearly seven hours when Frank nudged Wanda awake. She sat up and swung her legs off the bench seat where she had been napping. Kathy was sound asleep on the other bench seat.

The boat wasn't moving. The twin outboards were quietly idling and the outside floodlights had been turned off.

"Why have we stopped?" Wanda asked.

"We might have a little bit of trouble up ahead," Frank whispered. He was carrying a hunting rifle.

Enzo was sitting at the helm chair, loading shells into a sawed-off shotgun.

Wanda stood. She put on the gun belt and cinched up the buckle.

"Take this," Frank said, handing her a shotgun. "And put this on." He gave her a ball cap to wear. Frank was wearing a similar hat with the resort's logo on the front.

They went out the rear door and made their way along the side of the pilothouse.

Ignacio was standing near the bow, staring at the river ahead. He had a short barrel shotgun cradled in the crook of his right arm. He was also wearing a ball cap.

There were six fiery torches staggered about the water a hundred yards up ahead.

"Who are they?" Wanda asked.

"River pirates," Ignacio said.

"I thought that was only in Somalia."

"The bastards are everywhere," Frank said. "Once you get away from the big cities, there's no law on the river."

"How many do you think there are?"

Ignacio looked over at Wanda. "These river rats, maybe ten, a few more. The less there are, the less they have to share."

"Ignacio says our boat used to be a military vessel," Frank said. "We're thinking if we play it right, they might think we're the Brazilian Navy and might be too scared to attack."

"We're just going to bluff our way through?" Wanda asked.

"If we show enough force, they'll get out of our way."

James came around to the front of the pilothouse. He was wearing a ball cap and carrying a shotgun.

"I take it you know how to use that," Wanda said, unsure if she wanted someone next to her that wasn't properly trained in firearms.

"I go pheasant hunting all the time with my dad. Just don't tell Kathy. I don't want to upset her. You know, birds and all."

"Everyone stand ready, guns up," Frank said. "We want these jokers to think we're a military patrol boat." He looked back and saw Kathy had gotten up and was sitting in the chair next to Enzo.

Ignacio tapped on the window. Enzo pushed the throttle forward and the twin outboards roared, raising the bow for a moment before the fast-moving boat trimmed out.

The high-power halogen spotlights came on, lighting up the river ahead like a phosphorous bomb, blinding the ragtag bunch of cutthroats standing in their small boats. .

There were either two or three pirates to a boat; some of the men armed with handguns and machetes, a few with rifles. Each boat had a flaming torch on its bow and a small outboard motor clamped on the stern.

Enzo gunned the rescue boat straight down the middle of the river, creating a wide wake. He switched on the siren; the ear piecing wail an added distraction.

At first it seemed there wasn't going to be any opposition, but then one of the small boats started to zip over the water. Then another sped up until all six boats were racing toward the rescue boat.

Gun flashes started popping from the two nearest boats.

"Show them we mean business!" Frank yelled.

Frank took aim and shot at the first boat approaching. The bullet struck one of the pirates in the shoulder and he toppled out of the boat. The man steering the boat took a pot shot at Frank.

Wanda returned fire and blasted the man clear out of the motorboat.

Ignacio aimed his shotgun and pulled back both triggers at a man whose boat was almost alongside. The heavy-load buckshot punched the pirate out of the boat.

Another man threw a grappling hook, which caught onto the railing. He was climbing up the side of the rescue boat when James stepped up and smashed him in the face with his shotgun's butt stock.

Bullets zipped through the night air, striking the outside of the pilothouse.

Frank picked off two more pirates. More men fell into the water.

Another boat capsized.

The rescue boat broke through what was left of the blockade, and as it did, the craft left a wide swath of rough water behind, enough to upend two more of the raiders' boats.

Frank and Wanda held onto the side railing and edged to the rear of the rescue boat to make sure none of the pirates had managed to get on board and there were no boats following. Even though it was pitch black, they could see the trail of white water being churned up by the powerful outboard motors' propellers.

James stepped around the corner of the pilothouse. "I'm going to check on Kathy, make sure she's okay," he said and went inside.

"You think we've seen the last of them?" Wanda asked Frank as they stared out over the transom.

"I hope so. But if there's anything I've learned being in the Amazon, it's always to expect the unexpected."

"Well, that's not very reassuring."

26

Ally woke up to howling wind outside the bungalow. She sat up in bed and pulled back the mosquito netting. The bamboo slats on the high ceiling shook. Ally half-expected the thatched roof to be ripped off and she and Dillon to be sucked out and swept away by the storm. She could hear the heavy rain outside, pummeling the other guests' bungalows and the plank catwalks.

Dillon got out of his bed and padded barefoot over to Ally's bedside. "Why's it so loud?" he asked, rubbing the sleep from his eyes.

"It's a bad rainstorm," Ally replied.

"Does it have to rain all the time?"

"Jungles need a lot of water."

A part of the roof snapped, and when Ally looked up, she saw a shredded hole and a patch of dark gray sky. Rain began pouring into their room.

"Dilly, hurry and get dressed," Ally said as she reached for her clothes on the end of the bed.

The young boy scampered back to his bed and searched through his suitcase.

A blustering gust blew through the screened windows and overturned one of the rattan chairs. The walls trembled as the room swayed.

"We can't stay here," Ally shouted to her little brother. She'd gotten dressed and pulled on a poncho. She helped Dillon with his shirt, and then found his rain slicker.

Ally held Dillon's hand and opened the door. It was such a torrential downpour, Ally could have sworn they were standing at the base of a waterfall; it was coming down that hard.

"Are we going to drown?" Dillon asked worriedly.

"No, silly. We just have to go somewhere safe." Ally started to step out the door but the wind pushed her back into the room. She looked down at her brother. "You hold onto my hand tight. You hear?"

"Okey dokey," Dillon said, the hood of his slicker covering most of his face.

"Let's go," Ally shouted and leaned into the wind. She grabbed the handrail on the catwalk and pulled herself forward. The rain was blowing in her face so she had to squint. Debris flew everywhere as the wind battered the tree branches and slapped the leaves on the large fronds.

A figure was coming down the catwalk. He was waving and yelling something, but Ally couldn't hear above the storm.

It was Macky. He was wearing a white polo shirt and cargo shorts and was drenched to the bone.

"I came to get you," he yelled. "It's safer in the lobby."

"Thanks," Ally shouted back. She glanced over Macky's shoulder and saw something she had never seen before. A twisting cyclone hung from a turbulent cloud and was swirling over the river, heading straight for the resort.

"What is that?" she said to Macky and pointed.

He turned and took a step back. "Ah crap, it's a tornadic waterspout."

The funnel churned its way off the water and spun across the ground into the resort.

"Lie down flat!" Macky shouted.

They were only halfway across the catwalk and were out in the open. Ally and Dillon went on their bellies and Macky laid on top of them.

They covered their ears as the waterspout roared through the grounds of the resort, demolishing the bungalows in its path and dumping whatever it had sucked out of the river.

Ally could hear hundreds of splats and thumps all around her sounding like they were being bombarded by a heavy hail of indestructible water balloons.

The extension of the storm cloud crashed into the jungle and thundered off.

Like every tropical storm in the Amazon, it subsided as quickly as it had started, and the rain stopped.

"You two okay? Nobody hurt?" Macky asked as he got up.

"Yes, I think... Oh my God!" Ally shrieked when she saw the large snake slithering toward her head. She scrambled to her feet and pulled Dillon up.

Macky reached down, grabbed the snake by the tail, and flung it over the handrail.

The catwalk was teeming with thrashing fish and hopping frogs and glissading serpents, but mostly dead things that hadn't survived being blended in the mixer.

Even though Macky was barefoot, it didn't stop him from kicking at anything that seemed aggressive.

Ally looked down at the other end of the catwalk and saw Murilo, slowly advancing. He had a broom and was sweeping everything in his path off the catwalk onto the ground below.

She had never seen so many different colored frogs. They had brilliant markings, some dark blue, others flaming red, or burnt orange, or canary yellow. They were jumping over one another, croaking as they went.

Murilo was ten feet away when he stopped sweeping and yelled, "Don't touch little boy!"

Ally turned and saw Dillon running after a fluorescent-blue frog hopping away in the other direction.

"Dillon!" Macky shouted.

"What is it?" Ally asked.

"The frogs. They're poisonous. The brighter the color, the more deadlier they are."

The blue frog leaped onto an adjacent catwalk and disappeared around the corner.

Dillon dashed around the bend.

Ally and Macky took off after the boy.

When they rounded the corner, Dillon was standing over the blue frog and he was bending down to pick up the deadly amphibian.

"Dillon, stay away," Ally said, trying to warn her brother.

"Stop!" Macky yelled.

The boy's hand was mere inches from touching the frog's toxic skin.

Murilo suddenly appeared and swept the frog under the railing with his broom.

"Oh, thank God," Ally said and rushed over, grabbing Dillon in her arms.

"Hey, I wanted that," Dillon protested.

"Do you know what would have happened if you had touched that frog?" Ally asked sternly.

"I ain't scared of a silly wart."

"Little man, you have to be more careful," Macky said. "Listen to your sister."

"Do what?" Dillon said.

"Just don't be picking critters up until you check with me," Ally said. "Promise?"

Dillon gave her a sourpuss expression.

"Promise?" Ally asked again.

"Okay, I promise."

Murilo waved for them to follow him while he cleared a path down the catwalk to the resort's main building.

Walking alongside Macky and her little brother, Ally couldn't help thinking to herself, *All this excitement and we haven't even had breakfast.*

27

It was daybreak when Ryan and Jackie clambered down from their resting place. As soon as their boots touched the ground, they began brushing tiny insects off their arms and clothes.

"What are they?" Ryan said, stomping his boots to shake the bugs off of his pant legs. He flicked some from his shirt.

"Termites," Jackie replied. She was brushing them out of her hair with her fingers. "I should have known. The wood was too spongy."

"Well, at least it was comfortable. What time do you think it is?"

"How should I know?"

"Yeah, I guess that was a stupid question. Like it really matters."

Jackie looked at Ryan. "I'm sorry. I'm not really a morning person."

"That makes the two of us. So, what now?"

"Are you hungry?"

"Sure. What do you have in mind?"

"How about a continental breakfast?"

"Very funny," Ryan said.

"No, I'm serious. Come, I'll show you."

Ryan followed Jackie as she walked through an area of knee-high ferns.

She stopped and looked down at a rotted log. "You want to help me flip that over?"

Ryan got on one end as Jackie bent down and grabbed the other end.

"Okay, let's turn it on the count of three. One, two, three!"

The wood was so decayed it broke off in their hands as they rolled the log.

Underneath was damp, rich earth, and wriggling worms, grubs, crickets, and an assortment of bugs Ryan had never seen before.

"Quite the smorgasbord."

"That's our breakfast?" Ryan said.

"What did you expect, ham and eggs?"

"You've really eaten bugs before?"

"Last spring break, James and I went to Thailand. I was hoping to see an agile gibbon as they're on the endangered species list and James is a big advocate against deforestation, which was why the monkeys are becoming extinct. They're losing their natural habitat."

"You and James. Not Kathy?"

"James and I were going together at the time."

"So who dumped who?"

"Let's just say it was a mutual decision. Apparently he likes Kathy more. Anyway, while we were there, James and I tried some of the Thai cuisine. Fried insects are a big delicacy."

"Like what?"

"Well, grasshoppers are a little like pork rinds."

"Really."

"Yep. And then we had water bugs."

"You ate water bugs," Ryan said with disbelief.

"Yeah, they taste like licorice."

"Hmm." Ryan looked down at the assortment of creepy crawlers; nothing looked the least bit appetizing.

Jackie saw the uncomfortable look on Ryan's face. "They're high in protein. Until we can find anything better, I suggest you suck it up."

Ryan glanced over at Jackie and smirked. "How bad could it be?"

Jackie went first and picked up a six-inch-long worm. She cleaned off some of the dirt clinging to its slimy body. Without hesitation, she put one end in her mouth and slurped the rest between her lips like it was a long strand of spaghetti. After she swallowed, she smiled and said, "Your turn."

Ryan found a smaller-size worm. He didn't like the thought of swallowing it whole and it being alive, so he balled the worm, stuffed it in his mouth, and chewed it up.

He'd neglected to clean it so it was gritty and tasted somewhat salty. He tried not to over-think what he was doing and swallowed.

Looking over at Jackie, he saw her pop something in her mouth and crunch.

"What's that?" he asked.

"Cricket. Want some?" Jackie held out her hand and showed him half a dozen mashed up crickets on her palm.

"How many insects do we have to eat?"

"If you want to boost up your energy level, a bunch."

Ryan noticed something dangling out of the corner of Jackie's mouth; a cricket's leg, and it was still quivering.

He looked away, trying not to throw up. It was sweltering and he was feeling nauseated and the thought of eating a large helping of bugs was only making it worse, but he knew Jackie was right.

Time to suck it up!

28

Ben shoved the waterproof matches into his pocket and made sure he had put everything back in his rucksack.

The jungle was steamy after the last rain.

He'd brought along a plastic spray bottle of bug repellant, which seemed to be working fine as the flying insects weren't bothering him like before even though some insisted on buzzing into him on occasion like tiny dive bombers.

As he'd lost his cell phone in the river, he wasn't able to get a GPS satellite uplink on his location. He couldn't see the sun—though he could feel its sweltering heat—or the sky for that matter because of the thick tree canopy towering well over a hundred feet above his head.

He looked at the tree trunks, remembering the old saying about moss growing on the northern side of the tree. Even if it were true, it wasn't going to help him get his bearings in the rainforest. Due to the humid conditions, every tree trunk was covered completely by the green fungal growth.

If he listened hard enough, he could hear the faint sound of the fast flowing river somewhere off in the jungle. It was advisable, when lost, to follow a river as it would sooner or later lead to civilization. No matter how remote or hostile that may be.

Ben picked up his rucksack and hung one of the straps over his right shoulder. He chose a direction he thought paralleled the river and made his way through the jungle.

After traveling for more than an hour, Ben started to get the strange feeling he was being watched. Every time he thought there were eyes upon him, he would stop and look around.

Sure there were birds and other small creatures in the overhead branches, and insects galore, and the occasional skittering in the underbrush, but nothing presented a genuine threat.

Ben saw something out of the corner of his eye—a shadowy figure—darting between the trees. When he turned his head, whatever it had been was gone as if it hadn't really been there, like a ghost.

Again, he caught movement in his peripheral vision. This time he was sure what he saw, and it wasn't an animal.

It had been a very short person.

Ben thought about challenging whoever it was, but he didn't want to draw any unwanted attention even though he knew he was being stalked.

He stopped walking and stood still, listening to his surroundings. He could hear footfalls all around him.

Ben glanced to his right and saw a small, dark-skinned man step out of the foliage. He was completely naked and carried a bow with a strung arrow. A quiver of arrows hung on his back. His face was painted white and red, and he had a plume of blue-dyed hair, which made him look like an exotic bird.

Another naked man stepped out of the trees. He looked stoic and was armed with a long spear. One after another, his stalkers showed themselves, all of them naked and covered with different shades of body paint and strange headdresses.

Not one of them stood over four feet tall.

Ben soon realized he was surrounded by a band of pigmy warriors. He counted maybe twenty. There was no telling how many were hiding in the jungle.

He had studied countless Amazonian tribes but had never seen, let alone met, any pigmies.

Though they were shorter in stature, they looked exceptionally fierce, especially when banded together. Maybe it was their primitiveness, the fact they were all naked and lacked inhibitions, which meant they could be impulsively violent.

Even though their faces and skin were covered with bright dyes, not one of them looked the same. Ben had no idea if their appearances had any significant meaning to status or if it was just an individual preference; either way, their makeup made them scary looking.

If he had a weapon, he might have been tempted to reach for it but he didn't. He had no choice but to try diplomacy.

Ben raised his hands in a show of friendship.

The pigmies pulled back their bowstrings and thrust out their spears.

"I mean you no harm," Ben said, realizing how stupid he sounded—like an astronaut upon landing on a strange planet and greeting a hostile group of aliens.

Nonetheless, he stayed on the same tack. He cringed as he said, "I come in peace."

29

After Frank consulted the map one more time, he told Ignacio to bring the boat ashore. There was no way he could be certain, but judging from the last time Wanda was able to track Ryan, this bend in the river was their best guess to the young man's location.

Ignacio turned the helm and steered the front of the boat up onto the bank. Enzo jumped out and tied the bow line around a tree. He came back and climbed aboard.

"We're going to need someone to remain on the boat," Frank said.

"I'll stay with the boat," Enzo said.

"Good," Frank said.

"How will we know our way back?" Wanda asked.

Frank looked over at Ignacio. "What if Enzo sounds the siren, let's say, every four hours?"

Enzo nodded to Ignacio that he understood the request.

Frank looked at James and Kathy. "You two up for this?"

"Yes," Kathy said indignantly. "I'd do anything for Ben."

James gave her a questionable look.

"How about you, James?"

The young man looked at Frank. "You're going to need my help."

"Well, then, I guess it's settled," Frank said, and as the others were packing up their gear, he guided Wanda away so they could talk alone. "You know, this is going to be grueling."

"By grueling, you mean what?"

"I mean, this is going to be your worst nightmare."

"I don't care. This is my son we're talking about," Wanda told him. "Don't even go there."

"Sorry. You're right."

Soon everyone was assembling on the shore, hitching their packs on their shoulders, doing a last minute check to see if they had forgotten anything.

"Give us about fifteen minutes, and then give the siren a blast," Frank said to Enzo.

Enzo gazed at his wristwatch and gave Frank a nod.

"Let's head out." Frank took the lead with Wanda right behind him. Besides his pack, he also had the hunting rifle slung over one shoulder. Wanda had her sidearm and was also carrying a lightweight sawed-off shotgun.

James and Kathy followed next. James had a shotgun as well, but Kathy chose not to carry a weapon. Ignacio took up the rear to make sure no one got separated from the group, as there would likely be patches of forest so dense it would be easy to lose sight of a person.

Frank carried a machete in his right hand for blazing a trail, but so far he hadn't needed to use it. He'd been able to easily brush past the large palm leaves and hanging vines to make a path for the others. He could smell the sweet fragrance of the wild flowers and the bird-of-paradise.

He glanced back over his shoulder and saw Wanda admiring the beautiful orchids growing on the tree trunks. She even stopped to sniff one of the flowers.

A moth with a twelve-inch-long proboscis clung to the curved lip of the orchid and was gathering nectar from inside the deep narrow bowl.

"Look at the tongue on that thing," Wanda commented.

"That's Mother Nature for you," Frank said. "If she hadn't created these specialized pollinators, these orchids wouldn't exist."

Wanda took a moment and stared up through the branches of a tree that seemed to go on forever.

"That's a kapok tree, the tallest in the Amazon rainforest. They can grow up to two hundred feet," James said. "It's a pretty amazing species. The natives use the bark, resin and other parts of the tree to treat fever and dysentery."

"You don't say."

Everyone turned when they heard the sharp blast of the siren. It lasted for a few seconds and then went silent though there was a lingering echo but that soon faded away.

Frank looked at his watch. "Enzo's right on schedule."

30

"I still can't help feeling guilty," Ally said. She was sitting in the back of the canoe, dipping her paddle in the water.

"I know what you mean, but there's not much we can do. Murilo wouldn't let us help him with the cleanup as it's against the resort's rules to allow the guests to do staff work," Macky said, sitting up front and stroking his paddle through the water.

"He could have made an exception."

"Hey, we're on a vacation," Dillon piped in. He was wearing an orange lifejacket and sitting in the middle of the canoe with nothing to do but look out over the river and complain. He'd been antsy the entire morning; he didn't want to just sit around and do nothing.

Ally had come to her wits end having to listen to Dillon's constant whining and finally gave in to her little brother.

Macky had suggested going for a short canoe trip and got Dillon all hyped up about seeing some cool-looking fish like eels and armor-plated catfish.

If they were lucky, they might even spot some black caimans, which seemed likely, as there should be plenty of the freshwater alligators around seeing as the resort was named after them.

Dillon dragged his hand in the water, something Ally frowned upon and had repeatedly told him not to do.

"Keep your hand in the boat," Ally said.

"Why?" was always Dillon's reply.

"Because I said so."

Dillon kept his hand in the water.

"You wouldn't want a piranha to bite off a finger?" Ally said.

"Be more like a hand," Macky added.

"You're just trying to scare me," Dillon said. "It's not working."

Something brushed up against the bottom and rocked the canoe.

Ally lunged for Dillon, fearing he might be pulled from the boat. At the same time, Macky spun around in his seat.

The sudden movements on both their parts were enough to make the canoe tip and capsize, dumping them into the river.

Ally came up and swam over, grabbing the back of Dillon's life preserver.

Macky had one hand on the upturned hull. He was treading water and looking around. They weren't too far away from the shore.

"What was that?" Ally asked Macky.

"I just caught a glimpse. Pretty sure it was a caiman."

Without saying another word, Ally started to sidestroke with one arm as she towed Dillon behind her. Macky swam alongside the two, keeping his eyes open for any sign of a possible attack.

"Are you scared now?" Ally said angrily.

"I have to pee," Dillon shouted.

"Don't Dillon! Hold it in," Macky said. "We're almost there."

"But I really have to go!"

Soon their feet touched the river bottom and they were able to stand. They waded as fast as they could until they were completely out of the water and on the muddy bank.

"You can go pee now," Macky said.

Dillon ran off and stood facing a bush. His zipper sounded, followed by a heavy stream of pee.

"So what was that all about?" Ally asked Macky. "I don't swim in your toilet, so don't pee in my pool. Or should I say, river."

"I didn't mean to sound like an alarmist but it's better to be safe than sorry. There's a parasite fish, actually it's a very small catfish. The candiru. There have been cases where the fish have..."

"Have what?"

"They're small enough to swim up the urethra. They're drawn to urine."

"Oh my God, and they're real?" Ally said.

"Well, to be honest I think there's only been one case, and it was a woman. I just thought we better not chance it." Macky looked out over the water. "We're in enough trouble as it is."

Ally turned and saw their overturned canoe drifting downriver. "What do we do now?"

"We think our best bet is to stay right here. Sooner or later, Murilo will realize we haven't returned and he'll come looking for us."

"You're sure about that?"

"Look, it's not going to be dark for a few hours. He'll find us."

"Okay, if you say so," Ally said.

Dillon came over. He'd zipped part of his shirt in his pants.

Ally reached down, unzipped his fly, and corrected the problem.

"So, what are we going to do now?" Dillon asked, looking up eagerly at both Ally and Macky.

Ally rolled her eyes and let out a mournful sigh.

31

Murilo knew Ignacio wouldn't be pleased if he came back and saw the jungle litter all over the resort. The young man and woman remaining behind had insisted they help with the cleanup but Murilo refused their assistance, as it was not customary for guests to perform resort duties.

The storm had caused quite a mess. He'd cleared most of the catwalks and had made numerous trips carrying fallen tree branches to the edge of the jungle. Even though the afternoon heat was sweltering, Murilo hadn't broken a sweat. His tanned body was used to the harsh climate.

Carrying his broom, Murilo walked around to a different section of walkway he hadn't yet cleared away. As he stepped barefoot over the planks, he sensed danger lurking under a large palm leaf lying only a few feet away.

The pit viper shot out of its cover, fangs bared as it went for Murilo's right foot.

He stepped back, bringing the broom down, and pinned the snake's head with the coarse bristles. Reaching down, he grabbed the snake by the tail. Slowly, he raised the bristled-end of the broom.

And then, in one quick motion, Murilo snapped the snake like a bullwhip; breaking its vertebra column. The viper went limp in Murilo's hand and dangled onto the decking.

There was more work to be done on the next walkway. But, before he started sweeping, he needed to go down and discard the snake in the bushes. He'd lost count of how many frogs and snakes and other animals he had thrown into the jungle. It was of no concern to him. By tomorrow, the carcasses would all be gone, and the nocturnal predators would be back in their dens, licking the blood from their claws.

Murilo went down the stairs. He crossed over the short grass where the high brush ran up the sides of the trees.

He flung the snake into the bushes.

The big cat leapt out and pounced on Murilo. The two-hundred-pound jaguar latched onto Murilo with its sharp claws and tackled him to the ground. With jaws wide, the panther sunk its fangs into Murilo's skull.

Murilo's body twitched then went still.

The ambush had been quick and final.

With Murilo's head still in its mouth, the muscular jaguar dragged the dead man into the thicket.

After a moment, there was a loud roar from the jungle.

Then came the crunching of bone.

32

Ryan found a flat rock to hone the blade on his pocketknife. He worked up some spit and wetted the smooth stone. He passed the cutting edge of the knife back and forth, each pass making the blade sharper. When he was satisfied the steel was keen enough, he tested the blade and found it was as sharp as a razorblade when it sliced through a big leaf like it was a thin sheet of paper.

His throat was parched from having to constantly use up his spit. He noticed some rainwater had collected on a large umbrella-shaped leaf. He was about to channel some of the water down into his cupped hand when Jackie stopped him.

"You don't want to drink that," she warned. "Take a good look at what you almost drank."

Ryan leaned down and studied the trapped puddle. There were tiny, almost microscopic things squirming around in the water. "That's not good."

"Not good is right. You're probably looking at mosquito larvae and who knows what. This place is teeming with parasites."

"So what do we do? I'm dying of thirst," Ryan said.

"Well, now that you've sharpened your knife, I'll show you." Jackie looked around and pointed to some lianas hanging down from the trees. "Grab one of those vines, hold it up, and cut off the end."

Ryan held up a vine. He sliced through the end with his knife and was surprised to see water flow out of the vine like it was a garden hose and the spigot had just been turned on. He tilted his head under and let the water pour into his mouth. It was lukewarm but still tasted wonderful.

He cut another vine so Jackie could drink.

"So where did you learn that?" Ryan asked.

"James. He taught me quite a few things."

"Oh?"

"How to survive in the jungle. What do you think I was talking about?" Jackie said snidely.

"Well, you guys *were* going together," Ryan said with a smirk.

"Just follow me and shut up."

Jackie carefully studied the surrounding plants as they weaved their way through the rainforest. She stopped to inspect a broadleaf shrub. "Here, take the leaves and crumbled them up. Then rub it all over your face and neck. Be sure to get your arms and hands good."

"What's it called?" Ryan asked as he followed Jackie's instructions and tore off some leaves.

"I forget the name. Remember, James is the botanist. I just know what it looks like. Anyway, this should keep the bugs off."

"So it works like an insect repellant."

"That's right."

After they were through rubbing their skin with the leaves, Jackie led the way and after a few minutes, she stopped at another plant. She broke off a little portion of a leaf and handed it to Ryan.

"What's this for?"

"Just chew it. It works somewhat like the cinchona bark, which is used for making quinine to cure malaria."

"And this really works?"

"I guess. Sometimes I don't know whether to believe James or not. He's always been a bit of a showoff."

"So, for all we know, this plant could be poisonous," Ryan said, eyeing the bit of leaf.

"Or it could save you from dying a terrible death."

"I gotcha." Ryan put the portion of leaf in his mouth and chewed it up.

"Better shred some more up and keep them in your pocket. We need to dose up everyday."

"All right." After he filled one trouser pocket, he looked around and saw a stand of bamboo stalks almost twenty feet tall. He went over and grabbed a large shoot and bent it down to the ground. Using his pocketknife, he cut two six-foot lengths. Then he carved spearheads into each one.

Ryan handed Jackie a spear.

"Not bad," Jackie said, inspecting Ryan's work.

"Well, I am a carpenter apprentice by trade," Ryan said proudly.

"Oh, I would have thought you were a master spear maker."

"And I guess you're the local pharmacist."

"Looks like we have new professions," Jackie said.

Ryan hefted his spear. "Better add *hunter* to the list."

"You think you're going to be handy enough with that thing?"

"Time will tell," Ryan replied with a degree of confidence as he took the lead on their hike into the jungle.

33

It was late afternoon and they'd been sitting on the bank for almost two hours waiting for Murilo to show up. Certainly, he must have noticed their absence from the resort.

Macky was running out of interesting fish facts to amuse Dillon. He told Dillon there were over 2,200 species of fish in the Amazon region—and had even gone down an extensive list—but Dillon's attention span was very limited. He told the boy about the needle gar, the Amazon's freshwater version of the barracuda, and there were actual vampire fish with long fangs, but it was obvious the boy wasn't listening.

When Macky mentioned there were even sharks in the river, Dillon's ears perked up. "You mean like in *Jaws*?"

"Well, not as big as a great white," Macky had to confess.

"Does Murilo even know where we went?" Ally asked, interrupting their little tutorial and giving Macky an appreciated reprieve.

Macky was silent for a moment.

"You didn't tell him?"

"Sorry, I didn't think we were going to get stranded out here. He was busy."

"I'm hot. Can't I take this stupid thing off?" Dillon said, tugging at his life vest.

"No," Ally said firmly. "Not while we're near the water."

"I'm hungry," Dillon whined.

"Sure you are. We all are."

"We should just head back on our own," Macky said.

"You mean, hike through the jungle. It must be a least five miles back to the resort."

"Don't worry, we won't get lost. If we keep to the shoreline we'll find our way back before it gets dark."

"You really don't think he's coming?" Ally asked, not sure she wanted to walk all that way; especially knowing Dillon wouldn't be keen to traipsing through the jungle.

"It doesn't appear so."

"Okay." Ally looked over at Dillon. "Looks like we're going on a little hike."

Dillon made a face but didn't say anything.

At first it was easy to keep to the shoreline and follow the river, but it wasn't long before the bank was entangled with thick vines and buttress roots too tall to climb over, which forced them to detour inland.

After weaving through a dense patch of jungle, they came upon an open area of sand near a lagoon and a stream funneling down a rocky slope.

It was picturesque with the sunlight filtering through the trees.

"Too bad this isn't part of the tour," Macky said, gazing around at the splendorous setting.

"This would make the perfect postcard," Ally said.

Dillon started to walk across the sand when suddenly he stepped on something that cracked.

"What was that?" Ally said.

Macky and Ally walked over to Dillon.

"Lift your foot," Macky said.

Dillon raised his shoe revealing something smashed in the sand.

"What is that?" Ally asked.

Macky knelt on one knee and shoved the fractured eggshell around with his finger. "I don't think we should be here," he warned.

They heard another cracking sound and turned as a tiny head popped out of the sand. The creature cried out weakly with its first breath. Another infant broke out of its shell. Soon half a dozen newborn crocs were screeching as they clambered out of their cracked birthing incubators and onto the sand.

"Look, Ally! Baby alligators," Dillon shouted and ran to pick one up.

"We have to get out of here, and right now," Macky said.

Ally turned and saw the worried look on Macky's face. "What is it?"

"We're in the middle of a caiman nesting ground."

Dillon was holding a baby caiman.

The tiny croc was instinctually nipping at his fingers, thinking it was food.

A twelve-foot black caiman charged out of the brush. Two more came out from behind the trees.

The surface of the lagoon rippled. Four reptiles slowly appeared; the large eyes and their snouts then the bony ridges of their long bodies emerging as they swam for the beach.

Ally dashed over to Dillon. "Put that down!" She snatched the baby alligator out of Dillon's hand and placed it on the sand.

"Hey! That's mine," Dillon protested.

"Oh, yeah. Then tell that to its mother," Ally said and grabbed his hand.

Three caimans scrambled out of the water, propelling themselves across the sand with their powerful horn-ribbed tails. The crocodilians were over twelve feet long.

They crawled across the sand toward Dillon and Ally.

A caiman that had just swaggered out of the brush raised it upper jaw, revealing teeth as big as railroad spikes.

Another alligator hissed.

Macky looked for an opening.

The caimans were closing in.

"Run!" he yelled and scooped up Dillon.

Ally dashed after him, running through the gauntlet of fierce reptiles.

34

The warrior pigmies had formed a tight circle around Ben, and he knew at any moment they would attack. He was easily outnumbered twenty-to-one, and that wasn't taking into account how many were hiding out of sight, waiting for the signal to charge.

But then the mood of the Indians took a surprising turn.

They were grinning at him like he was the funniest thing they had ever seen.

The bow hunters unstrung their arrows and put them back in their quivers while the pigmies with the spears held their shafts upright, no longer in a threatening manner.

A few of the bolder pigmies came up to him and tugged at his shirt to see if it was his actual skin. They were laughing and jabbering in their native tongue, a dialect Ben was not familiar.

A gregarious warrior approached and offered to carry Ben's rucksack. At first he was apprehensive and didn't want to part with it, but after seeing how the pigmies were suddenly treating him so kindly, he didn't want to offend them and handed the pack over.

Other pigmies came out of the jungle to join in the celebration, doting over him like parishioners idolizing a god.

They grouped merrily around him, and before he knew it, he was in the middle of a precession marching through the jungle.

After an hour of parading through the rainforest, Ben was escorted into a large clearing and the pigmies' village, which comprised of a perimeter of a dozen thatched huts surrounding a longhouse, a common community dwelling arrangement used by most South American tribes.

Naked women and children scampered over and milled around Ben. Everyone was chanting and carrying on, so excited to have a guest in their village.

A few of the pigmy men ushered Ben toward the longhouse entrance. He had to duck his head as he went inside. The narrow room was gloomy so it was hard to see. A man ahead motioned for Ben to follow as they went into another portion of the structure.

Ben passed through what he thought to be a doorway. It was pitch dark as he came into the next room. He felt something brush past him.

A door closed shut.

Ben turned and reached out, touching a wooden barrier. He shoved but it was solid and wouldn't budge.

"Hey, let me out of here!"

He could hear voices and footfalls outside the longhouse.

Ben couldn't believe in a matter of seconds, his status had drastically changed from god to prisoner.

It was stifling in the enclosed room and the air smelt stale and pungent like something had been there for some time and had slowly rotted.

Ben took a few blind steps in the dark and hit an object with the toe of his boot.

He reached in his pants pocket and took out his waterproof matches. He flicked the phosphorus head of a match with his thumbnail.

The flame illuminated a small portion of the room, but it was enough for him to see what he had kicked on the ground.

It was a human skull.

Ben turned slowly and looked about the room. He was standing in the middle of a ring of thirty four-foot tall posts. At the base of each post was a skull, most likely of a defeated enemy.

The flame was getting down to almost burning his hand.

He gazed up at the top of a post and saw a small dark face with black hair and stitched up lips...

A shrunken head.

35

Even though they were hopelessly lost and had no idea where they were going, Ryan had to admit he liked the sense of adventure. He tried to imagine what it must have been like to be one of those early explorers of the New World he had often read about. Brave men who'd traveled afar to strange lands in hopes of discovering wealth beyond imagination so they could appease their king or queen, only to end up being killed in a strange land by a bunch of savages.

Striding through the jungle and carrying a spear, Ryan felt like a character straight out of an Edgar Rice Burroughs's novel. Especially whenever he would glance over at Jackie and see her wielding her own spear, and her lusty appearance with her damp hair and smudged face.

They'd covered a considerable amount of ground and seen many different aspects of the rainforest. The early morning mist had given the jungle a mystical look. As the day progressed, they crossed streambeds and saw different arrays of fauna, some parts too dense, other areas open and inviting.

The lush green was always in abundance, the moss-covered trees looming overhead like an emerald cathedral ceiling. They found migratory paths left by big animals and followed them until they petered out.

Early afternoon, they reached a lagoon under a waterfall. After a refreshing swim, they laid out on a rock to dry. Ryan tried his hand at spear fishing but hadn't quite got the knack. Jackie found some berries and they ate those instead.

They were hiking through a glen bordered by tall palms and buttress trees that had grown askew and looked like they were about to uproot and fall over when Jackie grabbed Ryan by the arm.

"What's wrong?" he asked and stopped walking.

"There's something up ahead."

Ryan looked at the foliage in front of them. He saw broad leaves and plenty of ferns and more greenery in the trees, but nothing he hadn't seen countless times before. "I don't see anything."

"Keep looking," Jackie insisted.

Ryan gazed at the foliage. He was about to break his concentration and tell Jackie she was seeing things when he saw it, too.

Two bulbous eyes with black pinpricked pupils; but nothing else.

It had been like staring intently at that test image of the white vase on a black background and then the brain suddenly recognizing the picture of two people facing each other.

"I see it," Ryan said in a low voice. "What do you think it is?"

"I don't know."

Ryan raised his spear. He took a step closer, hoping to get a better look and identify whatever it was but all he could make out were the creepy eyes, which were looking right at him.

Jackie pointed her spear forward.

"Let's just try and get around it, whatever the hell it is," Ryan said.

They had only taken a couple steps when the thing stepped out from the vegetation. Until it had actually moved, the camouflaged creature had blended in perfectly, invisible to the naked eye.

"Oh my God!" Jackie gasped.

"You got to be kidding me."

The giant praying mantis was as tall as Ryan.

When Ryan moved slightly, the large, triangular-shaped head swiveled in his direction. Standing on four legs, the mantis stood erect with its raptorial forelegs bent at the elbows, its wings tucked back against its stick-like body.

Ryan couldn't take his eyes off of the spines on the femurs and the huge two-toed claws.

"Be careful," Jackie warned. "Mantises are sexual cannibals."

"What?"

"The females bite the heads off the males after sex."

"I don't think I have to worry about that," Ryan said.

"That's also how they normally kill their prey."

"Here I thought you were trying to be funny."

Ryan sized up the mantis. Even though they were the same height, the giant bug was probably half his weight as its legs and body were spindly.

"Did you know they got this big?" Ryan said

"This has to be some kind of mutation," Jackie said.

"My stepfather, Frank, always boasts everything is bigger in the Amazon. I guess he wasn't kidding."

The mantis suddenly fanned out its wings, which made it looked twice as big. It stepped toward Ryan.

Ryan didn't back down and thrust his spear at the elongated body.

Jackie swung her spear like a baseball bat and clipped one of the mantis's stick legs. The giant bug's head pivoted on its long neck and it glared at Jackie.

"Get out of here!" Ryan yelled.

The praying mantis hissed, and in a grand display, fluttered its wings like an enormous dragonfly and took off.

Ryan and Jackie ducked as the giant insect flew over their heads.

"Wow, that was really something," Ryan said as he watched the mantis disappear into the trees.

"I'll say."

"Let's just pray there aren't any more of them," Ryan said with a grin.

Jackie smirked and shook her head. "Now, who's trying to be funny?"

36

Frank heard the faint shrill of the rescue boat's siren. They were so far away it was difficult to judge the true direction, but he was glad Enzo was still sounding the alarm at four-hour intervals.

"Let me know when you want to rest," he called over his shoulder.

"I'm fine, though a shower would be great," Wanda said, walking a few steps behind.

James and Kathy were talking amongst themselves while Ignacio trudged after them with his shotgun ready, always vigilant of their surroundings.

Frank put his hand up for everyone to stop.

"What is it?" Wanda asked.

"There's something moving over there in the grass." Frank motioned for Ignacio to come join him. Ignacio rushed up.

"Maybe a boa," Frank said, and Ignacio nodded.

The two men waded through the grass then froze when they saw the long creature, not slithering like a snake, but marching on hundreds of legs.

"It's an enormous centipede," Frank said, loud enough so the others could hear.

"Are you serious?" Wanda said.

"Look for yourself."

Wanda approached warily and stood next to Frank. "Oh my God. It has to be over eight feet long."

James and Kathy hurried over to take a look.

"That must be a Guinness record," James said.

"What about those gigantic centipedes they discovered on that island in the Philippines last year?" Kathy said. "Weren't they even bigger?"

"Who knows?" James said. "After they evacuated everyone off the island, the U.S. Air Force came in and incinerated the entire island with napalm."

They watched awestruck as the enormous centipede weaved through the grass and scuttled into the underbrush.

"That's got to be the biggest centipede ever, eh Frank?" James said.

"Could very well be, but you never know."

"What do you mean?"

"Ever hear of Raymond Trodderman?"

"Sure, he was an entomologist, such as yourself. Didn't he die in an airplane crash?"

"That's right. He had a journal. In it, he had recorded finding a species like you just saw, only much bigger, in the Amazon."

"And you think that might be *here*?"

"Could be."

"And where's this journal now?" James asked.

"Unfortunately, it was destroyed."

"That's a shame," Kathy said. "I'll bet there were some great discoveries in that journal."

"There were," Frank said.

"What, you got to read it?" James asked.

"Parts, not all. But he did mention finding a plant."

"What does it look like?"

"I don't know as there weren't any pictures. The only thing he noted was that it was so magnificent, that if you saw it, you'd know you found it."

"So what was so special about this mysterious plant?"

"He had a notion that it was *the* cure," Frank said.

"Cure for what?" James asked.

"The big C. Cancer."

James's eyes lit up like someone had just handed him a billion dollars.

37

Ben felt around in the dark. He tore a leafy stalk from the thatched ceiling and balled up the end. He lit another match and touched the flame to his improvised torch, which burned brightly.

He took a closer look at the shrunken head on top of the post to appraise the craftsmanship. The head was the size of a big navel orange. He could make out the facial features of the closed eyelids and the flat nose and the lips of the mouth sewn together with twine.

It was terrifying to think in the very near future his head would be on one of these posts.

He felt sick to his stomach, especially when he thought back to an article he had read about the process. After the decapitation, his skin would be sliced from his skull and boiled in a pot with different plants to make the skin shrink. Afterward it would be left to dry, then stuffed with hot stones to further shrink his head and then stitched up.

Small cords would be sewn on the top of his miniaturized head so it could be worn around someone's waist.

Ben wondered which of the pigmies would be the honored warrior performing a ritual dance, dangling the white man's head.

The only tribes in the Amazon in the habit of shrinking the heads of their enemy were the Jivaro, and as far as he knew, they were not pigmies. Which could mean only one thing. His captors were of an indigenous tribe unknown to the civilized world.

Ever since he began studying anthropology, his biggest dream was to document a new culture of people; and here he was, a captive guest in their village.

If only there was a way he could convince them he was a great warrior to be revered rather than a mere fool they had easily tricked.

He placed the torch on the ground and let it slowly burn in the dirt.

His shadow shone eerily on the hut wall.

He saw a sliver of light, bent down, and peered through the slight opening in the wall.

Outside, women and children were congregated as if expecting a major event to take place. Men were carrying wood and stoking a big fire while a few women set up Y-shaped stands on each side of the pit.

Two pigmies carried a long pole and set it on the yokes just above the flames.

Ben realized what he was observing.

They had just erected a rotisserie.

It wasn't bad enough they were headhunters; they had to be cannibals, too?

38

Ally saw Macky sidestep the snapping jaws of a caiman and nearly go down, but he held onto Dillon. When the crocodilian turned, Ally jumped over its back as though she were leaping over a low hurdle. Macky stumbled across the sand but stayed on his feet and picked up the pace into a determined jog.

Ally snuck a quick glance over her shoulder. Most of the caimans had already turned to resume guard over their newborns. She was pretty sure they were no longer a threat and were outside of the nesting ground and was about to slow down when a humongous caiman burst out of the short grass. It was larger than the others, over sixteen feet and extremely fast as it raced after them on its stubby legs.

"Why is it still chasing us?" Ally hollered.

Macky kept running and turned his head to look back. "That must be a bull. He's making sure we never come back."

"So how long is he going to keep chasing us?"

"I don't know." Macky suddenly cried out and disappeared off the path.

Ally tried to stop in time but she was going too fast and flew off the steep embankment. She splashed down into the water and went under for a moment. She came up and saw Macky a few feet away. Dillon was floating nearby but didn't appear to be hurt. Ally was thankful she'd insisted he keep on his life preserver.

They had landed in a pond half the size of a football field. Large, green lily pads floated on the surface. Ally looked around and saw most of the surrounding shoreline was about eight feet up from the water with sheer walls of thick intertwined vines that could be used to scale up. There was one sandy bank across the pond raised in a mound with visible burrow holes.

Ally swam over to Macky who was treading water and still able to hold onto Dillon. "What now?"

But before Macky could reply they heard a loud commotion as the black caiman slid down the embankment, snout first and slammed into the water.

"This way!" Macky yelled. He swam frantically with one hand, kicking his feet as he towed Dillon through the lily pads. Ally did the sidestroke so she could keep an eye on their pursuer.

"Ally, look out!" Dillon yelled when the crown of the black head emerged twenty feet behind them.

Ally watched in horror as the entire body and tail began to show.

Macky and Ally poured it on and churned up the water with their feet.

Reaching the shore, Macky grabbed hold of a vine and hoisted Dillon out of the water. "You've got to climb up," he instructed the boy.

Dillon reached for a vine but his hands were wet and he slipped. Macky boosted him back up, and this time, Dillon was able to seize a vine and grapple another and start his ascent.

Macky was waiting for her to go next but time was running out. "Go!" she yelled, and clutched a vine.

The caiman was fifteen feet away. Raising its upper jaw.

Ally tried pushing up with her feet but her right boot got snagged in a coil of roots. The only way for her to get loose was to slip back down.

Macky snatched a vine to pull himself up but when he saw Ally was having trouble, he extended his hand. "Here, let me help you."

"I'm stuck." Ally heard a loud splash. She peeked over her shoulder and saw a brown shorthaired animal had jumped into the pond. Four more similar-looking thick-bodied creatures come out of the burrow holes on the sandy bank and entered the water.

Ally looked up at Macky. "What are those?"

"Giant otters," Macky replied. "Seems like we've not only stumbled into a caiman's nesting ground, now we're trespassing through giant otter territory."

"Oh my God."

"But it can be a good thing."

Dillon had climbed up the vines like a little monkey and was already at the top.

Ally watched the five otters torpedo through the water. Judging by the one she saw jump in the water they were all probably around six feet long, more than a hundred pounds each—but certainly no match against a 1400-pound alligator.

"They don't have a chance," Ally said, still trying to dislodge her boot from the underwater vine.

"Oh, you'd be surprised what these guys can do," Macky said.

The caiman must have sensed the vibrations in the water as it began to turn its body to face the approaching otters head-on. But instead of a full frontal assault, the otters dove under the surface.

An otter's ball-shaped head popped out of the water directly in front of the caiman. The gator slowly opened its mouth.

The other four otters burst out of the water and were all over the caiman, climbing on its ridged back. The smaller creatures were fierce as a group and sank their sharp incisors deep into the reptilian's armored flesh. As the croc tried to shake off its tormentors it went into a death roll and flipped around in the water thrashing its tail, making the mistake of exposing the softer tissue of its underbelly.

Ally could hear the otters screeching as they harassed the formidable interloper, forcing it toward the far embankment.

Cornering the caiman against the shore, three of the otters pinned the larger animal down while the other two otters set about biting through the reptilian's neck to finish it off.

Ally tugged again and finally freed her boot. She grappled with the vines and pulled herself up. She gazed across the pond and watched as a massive amount of blood pooled to the surface, staining the lily pads.

"They just saved our lives."

"Ally, those otters could care less. They were just protecting their own."

39

Enzo stepped out of the jungle onto the shore. He climbed aboard the rescue boat and went inside the pilothouse. He put the cluster of bananas and a bagful of herbs and berries he had collected, on one of the bench seats. He checked the clock on the console by the helm. It was near time to sound the siren so he twisted the knob and gave the alarm a shrill shriek then switched it off.

He glanced out the window and saw a bevy of quail burst out of the brush. Every time he blasted the siren, it always scared something.

He stepped out of the wheelhouse and went aft to check his drop lines. He had half a dozen draped over the side, thin filaments with barbed hooks and segments of worms on the ends, enough to attract small fish as he was only fending for himself and didn't need much.

Unlike Murilo, who had grown accustomed to resort living and being around people, Enzo preferred his solitude, which is why he had volunteered to stay with the boat.

He pulled up one line after the other and dropped the small silver fish into a pail.

Enzo heard an echoing shriek and saw a twenty-pound harpy eagle with a seven-foot wingspan swoop over the middle of the river. Its gray head was crowned with a double crest and had a broad black band across its upper chest with a full plumage of black and white slate feathers.

A live monkey dangled from the raptor's talons.

Enzo watched the mighty bird soar away into the darkening sky.

He carried the pail to the forward deck and fired up the cook stove.

An hour later he had finished his meal and had made sure he hadn't left any food scraps lying around that might attract any unwanted predators onto the boat. He went inside the pilothouse to relax in the cabin and escape the bothersome bugs.

At night, Enzo kept only a single low-wattage light on so as not draw on the battery. He waited until it was time and sounded the siren. He switched off the light and stretched out on one of the bench seats.

He had almost fallen asleep when he felt a thump against the hull. He heard voices outside.

Slipping off the bench seat, Enzo stayed low and crept over to the window.

A full moon was shining in the night sky and Enzo could make out three silhouettes in a small boat alongside.

He knew right away who they were. He chastised himself for being so stupid. He'd brought the pirates right to him by sounding the siren.

The first pirate stepped out of the small boat, carrying a machete, and climbed aboard. The next man was armed with a rifle. Enzo couldn't tell if the last man had a weapon as he was still seated by the outboard motor.

Enzo looked around in the dark for his shotgun. He'd left it by the door. If the first intruder were to come inside, he'd surely brush up against the barrel leaning against the panel. Enzo didn't like the idea of being trapped inside the cabin with only one way out.

He got down on his hands and knees and scampered between the bench seats but as he got closer to his shotgun, the door slowly opened. Enzo would have to reach in front of the open doorway to grab his gun, which might mean losing an arm to a machete.

Instead, he reached down for his knife and pulled it slowly out of the sheath.

He tucked himself in the corner and waited for the man to enter the cabin.

A bare foot stepped in.

Enzo brought his knife down and stabbed the man's foot. He yanked out the blade as the man screamed. He jumped to his feet and stabbed the man in the chest once then pulled out the blade and shoved it back into his heart.

The second man was already on deck and charging the door.

Enzo pushed the man he had just stabbed to death into the other pirate. He reached over and grabbed his sawed-off shotgun. The man with the rifle had fallen with the dead man on top of him and was just pushing the corpse away when Enzo shot him in the face.

Turning, Enzo saw the man in the small boat tugging on the starter rope in an attempt to escape. He shot the man where he sat and watched him slump over the motor.

Enzo dragged a dead pirate over to the gunwale and dumped his body over the side into the motorized dugout. He went back and tossed in the other man so all three were sprawled in the boat.

He opened the cap on a five-gallon gasoline can and poured the contents over the bodies and most of the boat. Using a long-handle fishing gaff, Enzo pushed the boat adrift. He waited until the canoe was twenty feet away and then fired a projectile from his flare gun at the gasoline-doused boat. The craft erupted into a funeral pyre and burned bright, lighting up the shoreline and the surrounding jungle.

Enzo watched the blaze on the river until it became bubbling smoke and sank with a loud hiss.

He walked back inside the cabin and looked at the clock.

Soon it would be time to sound the siren again.

40

Frank leaned over and chucked some more wood into the campfire. James and Kathy had already fallen asleep, and Ignacio was somewhere not too far off, combing the immediate area and staying vigilant.

Frank sat back against a boulder and looked over at Wanda. She was staring pensively at the mesmerizing flames.

"How're you doing?" he asked. It had been a long day and he could tell she was tired by the strained look on her face.

"I'm all right."

"He's out there. We'll find him," Frank said. He thought by giving her constant reassurances he could convince her not to give up hope and somehow put her mind at ease, though deep down he was beginning to have his own doubts.

Wanda turned and looked at Frank. "Will we?"

"You have to have faith."

"Right now, I'm not really big on faith." Wanda picked a stick up from the ground and waved it at the fire. "Do you think Ally and Dillon are okay?"

"They're fine. Murilo won't let anything happen to them. Let's just concentrate on Ryan."

Frank thought he heard the distant chirp of the siren. It was difficult to be sure the way sound could play tricks in the night. For all he knew it was a dumb bird.

Wanda tapped the stick on her knee. "I have a bad feeling. It's been three days since we've seen him and now we're not getting a signal from his phone."

"Ben and Jackie have been here more than once. Between them I think they have enough survival skills to have made it this far. You just have to think positive."

"Think positive, right."

"Did you know there's an insect that can clone itself and reproduce without mating?"

"What *are* you talking about?"

"It's called a walking stick."

"And why is this relevant?"

"Because you're holding one right now."

Wanda looked at the stick in her hand and saw it had four legs. "Oh, jeez," she said and flung it away. "My God, this place."

Ignacio stepped out of the brush. He had his shotgun cradled across the crooks of both arms and stood on the opposite side of the campfire. His shadow made him look like a giant cast on the backdrop of the jungle.

Another shadow crept toward Ignacio's silhouette.

It was huge and bulbous and crawling straight for Ignacio.

Wanda yelled, "Ignacio!"

Frank jumped to his feet.

Ignacio looked down at the ground and began to laugh.

James and Kathy must have heard Wanda's outburst because they were rushing over to the campfire. "What is it?" James asked, groggy-eyed. Kathy was clutching his arm.

Frank dropped to one knee as Wanda came up behind him.

"What in the world is that?" Wanda asked.

"That," Frank said, "is an assassination bug." Even though the insect was only two inches long, the glowing fire made its shadow look like an enormous abomination of twisted appendages straight out of *Dante's Inferno*. "It piles dead ants on its back to make it look larger and intimidating."

Wanda shook her weary head. "Walking sticks, assassination bugs, what next?"

Everyone turned suddenly when a man stumbled out of the jungle and fell to his knees in front of the campfire. The Indian's body was slashed with ribbon cuts. His eyes were wide as saucers and he looked completely mad. He kept mumbling and stared into the fire.

Ignacio crouched beside the crazed man in an attempt to communicate.

After a moment, Frank asked, "Any idea what he's saying?"

Ignacio glanced up with an incomprehensive look. "Only that his village was attacked by demons, and his name is Diogo."

41

Ryan had watched a few Bear Grylls episodes where the wilderness survivalist would take a famous celebrity to a remote, rugged location and they would rough it for a few days. Grylls had a way of getting the other person to open up and reveal something private about their life. Ryan thought back and tried to remember one of Grylls's key survival tactics—how to build a fire—which wasn't going to be much use to Ryan, as Grylls used a magnesium-flint fire starter tool.

Which left Ryan with only two choices.

He could rub two sticks vigorously together and create enough friction to get the wood to burn, or he could strike his knife blade on a flinty rock fast enough to generate sparks.

As he had recently sharpened his knife, he was worried he might wear away the metal. The worst scenario he might snap the blade.

He asked Jackie to scout around for kindling, anything dry enough that might catch fire easily. She came back with a handful of bark chips and clumps of moss.

"That should work," Ryan said. He'd already cleared a small patch of ground and placed a flat piece of wood on the dirt inside a fire pit he'd arranged with rocks, and had found two foot-long sticks perfect for the task.

Jackie placed the moss loosely on the flat surface of the wood.

"Do your stuff," she said.

Ryan grabbed both sticks and began rubbing the ends together over the moss. It was strenuous work but he kept at it. Soon he was surprised to see a tendril of smoke. He rubbed even harder and saw a tiny flame igniting the tinder bundle.

Jackie added more moss and a few thin pieces of bark as Ryan built a teepee of wood strips and branches over the blaze.

Soon they had a nice fire they could cook on.

"You're sure this is okay to eat?" Ryan asked. He was referring to the giant snail they had found. He was used to seeing the small garden-variety type no larger than a ping-pong ball, not a monster the size of a halved bowling ball. Even Jackie was a little surprised at how big it was.

"There's always the snake," Jackie said, nodding to the dead serpent by the fire she had killed earlier with her spear. She'd taken the initiative and skinned it with Ryan's knife, even chopping it up into four-inch chunks for easier consumption.

Ryan added more wood to the fire. He picked up the snail, figuring it had to weigh at least two pounds, and placed it on the hot rocks. Still alive, the snail's muscular foot sizzled as it tried to escape but Ryan kept it stationary with a stick and flipped it over so it would cook in the shell, much like in its own stewing pot.

Jackie threw on the cutup snake, which crackled like bacon.

As they watched their dinner cook, Ryan sat back and said, "You know, I can't stop thinking about that praying mantis. What could have caused it to get so big?"

"My guess, it's the result of some kind of DNA breakdown. Maybe caused by some chemical."

"So you're saying, someone is using the jungle as a toxic dumping ground."

"Sure, why not."

"Sounds more like a conspiracy theory."

"Okay. What about radiation? I'm sure there are radium deposits all over this jungle."

"So now we're talking Godzilla?"

"I'm being serious."

"Did you ever see the movie *The Mysterious Island*?"

"I don't believe so."

"It's about this group of people who get marooned on this deserted island. I watched it with my little brother. It's got all these great Ray Harryhausen special effects where they're getting attacked by giant crabs and humongous bees."

"So."

"Kind of like this place, wouldn't you say?"

"Let's hope not." Jackie took her stick and rolled the huge snail off the coals. She picked the cooked snake strips out of the fire and put each piece onto a platter-sized leaf as a serving dish. She fanned a piece before putting it in her mouth.

Ryan used his stick, dug out a piece of snail meat, and took a bite.

It wasn't half bad.

42

Ben knew his time was up when he peered through the slit in the wall and saw a small group of pigmy men headed for the front of the longhouse. It was dark outside except for around the fire pit. The elders, women, and children were staring into the flames, their naked bodies aglow.

He could hear the men removing the length of timber used to brace the door shut.

Any second, and they would be entering the room to collect him.

He wasn't sure if they would kill him right away. Mostly likely it wouldn't be in the trophy room, which meant they would drag him outside and display him in front of the entire village in a sacrificial, ritual beheading.

The door swung open.

Six small figures stood in the gloomy doorway. They began to enter the dark room, but as they did, they stumbled and fell over one another.

Ben flicked the head on a match with his thumbnail and lit a large torch in his other hand. He touched the flame to the ceiling of the thatched roof.

The pigmies kept falling over the mound of skulls and shrunken heads he'd piled in front of the doorway. Ben had even pulled some posts out of the ground and stacked them haphazardly making the crossing even more difficult.

The fire spread quickly and licked down the walls in a bright blaze.

He'd taken his shirt off and wrapped it around his nose and mouth for a mask as the room was filling up with smoke, which stung his already watery eyes.

One of the warriors cleared the obstacles and came at Ben with a spear.

Ben shoved the flaming torch into his face. The pigmy screamed and fell back onto the jumble of skulls, tiny heads, and posts, and added to the stumbling block.

The frightened pigmies turned and clambered back in the other direction. Ben wanted to think it was because they had finally met their match—him being a fierce warrior—but knew they were just too petrified of being burned to death.

Either way, Ben knew he had only one chance and this was it.

Most of one wall was completely engulfed in flames and parts of it were already falling apart. The heat was intense and all he could see was smoke. If he didn't get out now, he never would.

Ben charged through the wall.

And burst out the other side. He was covered with burning embers but there was no time to brush them off as he ran like hell.

He wished there was time to search for his rucksack, but there wasn't. He'd have to leave his supplies behind.

He had to get as far away as possible. He could hear screaming and hollering behind him. Setting the longhouse on fire had been a wise diversion and would hopefully give him a good headstart.

He could see in the dark and was thankful for the full moon even though it meant he'd be easier to find. Dashing through the evergreen rainforest, he swatted palm leaves and low hanging branches out of his way. Twice he almost tripped on exposed roots and fell, but he managed to stay on his feet and kept running.

He had never once looked back and had covered some considerable ground when he had to stop because he was so winded. He leaned forward and placed his hands on his knees. Gasping, he took in a couple full breaths and tried to steady his breathing.

He stood erect and listened. He heard the same insidious wildlife drone that always seemed to be playing, reminding him of background sounds for a meditation session.

Accompanied by footfalls racing toward him through the jungle.

Even though his legs felt weak and rubbery, he knew he had to keep going if he wanted to stay alive. He ran as fast as his tired legs could carry him. If he had to, he would stop and fight, even though to do so would be suicide.

He pushed himself and stumbled forward.

Then the ground went out from under him and he crashed through the leaves.

43

Luckily, Mackey had thought to bring along his penlight, which had been in his pocket. After taking it apart and letting the inside dry out, he put the battery back in and it worked like a charm. It gave off enough illumination to see maybe ten feet in front of him. Once in awhile, the silver beams of the full moon would filter down through the treetops onto the jungle floor.

"How much farther to the resort?" Ally asked, walking behind him. She was carrying Dillon as he had fallen asleep.

"You want me to carry him for a bit?" Macky stopped and turned, pointing the beam at the ground.

"What if we just stop for a moment?"

"Fine by me."

Ally set Dillon on the ground beside a large tree. As soon as she propped her little brother against the trunk, he woke up. "Are we there yet?"

"No, Dilly." Ally's shoulders ached from lugging the sixty-pound boy. She shook out her arms to relax the muscles much like she would prior to a race at a track meet.

"Well, now that Dillon's awake, maybe we can pick up the pace," Macky said.

"You mean run?" Dillon frowned at Macky.

"I don't think we'll be doing that."

Something moved in the underbrush.

"What was that?" Ally said with alarm.

They could hear it snorting and rooting about the ground.

Mackey panned his penlight and frightened a brown, shorthaired animal enough to make it start squealing.

"Hey, little piggy," Dillon said and ran to grab the runt that couldn't have weighed more than ten pounds.

"Dillon, no!" Macky yelled.

"Macky, it's only a piglet," Ally said, suggesting Macky was over reacting.

"You don't understand, that's not a pig. It's a peccary. And peccaries generally travel in herds. I'm thinking this little fellow must have wandered off and got lost."

"Does that mean we can keep him?" Dillon said. He'd managed to grab the peccary by one of its hind legs, which made it squeal even louder.

"Dillon, let it go before—" Macky turned to the approaching sound of hooves stampeding through the jungle. "Must be the whole damn herd."

Macky handed Ally the penlight. "Go, I'll follow."

Ally took the small flashlight and went to grab Dillon's hand but her brother was still wrestling with the baby peccary. "You heard Macky. Let it go!"

Dillon released the screaming animal and it darted into the shrubs.

"Run!" Macky shouted.

They fled through the trees. Macky looked back over his shoulder and saw three large adult peccaries racing after them. They were slender-legged animals with powerful bodies, weighing about eighty pounds apiece, and were fast runners.

Even though the peccaries were omnivores, they were still wild animals capable of inflecting serious injuries and were fierce when attacking as a group.

He remembered Jackie telling him how peccaries sharpened their eyeteeth just by opening and closing their mouths and rubbing their incisors against their bottom teeth, giving them the ability to crush hard seeds and slice through roots.

Macky knew they weren't going to be able to outrun the murderous pack.

"We can't stay on the ground," he yelled.

Ally was running half speed so Dillon could keep up. She waved her hand she understood.

Macky could hear the pack right on his heels.

Ally shined the penlight beam onto a fallen tree that had uprooted and was leaning on another tree forming a ramp.

"Up there," Macky shouted.

Ally pushed Dillon ahead of her as they hustled up the slanted trunk, grabbing branches as they climbed to get higher.

Macky was right behind them. He scrambled up the moss-covered bark and almost slipped off but kept shimmying up.

They kept climbing until they had reached a height of thirty feet above the ground.

One of the adult peccaries tried to scale the fallen tree but the bark was too slippery and it slid off, falling on its side. The animal got back on its feet and shook its long-haired body.

More peccaries appeared and gathered around the base of the fallen tree.

Macky asked Ally for the penlight and he shined the beam down on the ground.

He counted ten adults and a dozen small ones. By the way they were hanging around, he didn't figure they were going to leave anytime soon.

"I think we're going to be here for awhile," he said, as they tried to make themselves comfortable in an indentation between two large boughs.

Dillon put his head on Ally's lap. She stroked his hair as he went off to sleep.

Macky looked down at the peccaries. "Ever get the strange feeling we're not welcome?" He turned to Ally to get her reaction but she, too, had dozed off.

He turned off the penlight.

He stretched out the best he could and closed his eyes. He listened to the snorting peccaries tearing up the ground below with their snouts, and before he knew it, he had joined Ally and Dillon and had drifted off.

44

As soon as they broke camp it began to pour rain, and everyone ducked under the giant palm leaves for cover. The deluge lasted for more than ten minutes.

Wanda and Frank were sharing the same leafy shelter. "You'd think after a good rain, it would cool things down."

"I know," Frank said. "It just adds more moisture to the air and makes you sweat more."

James and Kathy walked over.

"Did you guys get much sleep last night?" Kathy asked. "I sure didn't."

"You think he's crazy?" James said.

"Diogo?" Frank shrugged his shoulders and looked at Wanda.

"He definitely saw something that has him terrified," Wanda said.

"He wouldn't stop jabbering," Kathy said.

"I think Ignacio was finally able to get through to him."

They looked over and saw Diogo standing with Ignacio. The resort guide had treated the man's cuts and convinced him to come with them, which seemed to console Diogo, as he wasn't as distraught and fretful.

Frank cocked his head as a sound came faintly through the trees. He hoped it was the siren.

"Did you guys hear that?" Kathy said. "That's a macaw mating call."

"Okay everybody, time to head out." Frank waved everyone forward.

For the next two hours, they journeyed through the steamy rainforest. It was the hottest day since they had left the resort. And the going seemed tougher as now Frank and Ignacio had to use their machetes to clear a pathway through the dense jungle.

Frank was relieved when he finally broke out of the thick vegetation and brought the group into a grassy meadow with robust flowers, bordered with surrounding fan-shaped palms.

"Let's take a fifteen-minute break," Frank said.

"Sounds good to me," Wanda agreed and shrugged out of her backpack.

James and Kathy took off their packs and found a place to sit.

Ignacio and Diogo stood next to the gray-green trunk of a royal palm. Ignacio took a handful of nuts out of his bag and shared them with the Indian.

A few minutes passed.

Wanda waved her hand in front of her face to brush away a persistent swarm of gnats. She looked down at the ground and saw a parade of ants marching through the grass like they were off to pay someone a visit or perhaps returning back to their colony.

She looked over at a tall patch of grass and could see that something was moving through the sedge. "Frank?"

"Yeah," he replied, rummaging in his bag for something to eat.

"I think we're being stalked."

Frank looked up. "What?"

"Over there," Wanda said and pointed.

Frank slowly reached for his rifle.

James must have overheard Wanda because he had picked up his shotgun and was standing in front of Kathy.

"Ignacio!" Frank used the muzzle of his rifle to indicate that there was a predator in the tall grass. Ignacio closed the breech on his shotgun and thumbed back the hammers.

The herbage slowly parted.

Frank was familiar with the creature that stepped out of the grass as he had crossed paths with this particular species many times. Only this one was incredible.

"Oh my God, Frank. What the hell is that thing?" Wanda gasped.

"It's an ant-mimicking spider."

"And they get that big?"

"No, nothing like this." Frank had never seen anything like it before. The arachnid was enormous and had to be four feet tall and at least eight feet long. It had four black-globed eyes and its body was covered with silver, bristly hairs.

"Those aren't antennae near its head," Frank said. "Those are actually its front legs. Eight legs are typical of spiders. Ants only have six."

"But why pretend to be an ant?" Wanda asked unable to take her eyes off of the super-sized spider.

"Just part of the natural design of things I guess. That and they can pretty much reclassify themselves as a predator, or prey for that matter."

"Is it going to attack?" Kathy said, hiding behind James.

"I think we should be worried."

Diogo had been standing on the other side of the royal palm and hadn't seen the giant spider until he stepped around the trunk. As soon as he laid eyes on the creature he immediately started to scream.

"Ignacio, tell him to be quiet," Frank snapped. He turned to Wanda. "Watch out, these things can—"

The ant-mimicking spider jumped across the clearing in one swoop and came down on top of Diogo. The giant arachnid seized the small man and sank its fangs into his shoulder.

Frank aimed his rifle and shot the spider through the head. Ignacio and James leveled their shotguns and blew gaping holes in its body. The spider collapsed on top of Diogo's still body.

Everyone gathered around for a closer look.

Diogo's eyes were bugged out and his face was swollen like a puffer fish. All the veins in his neck and chest bulged on the surface of his skin like a competing bodybuilder.

"He was probably injected with enough venom to kill an elephant." Frank looked at the others. "Well, I guess now we know what Diogo was so afraid of."

45

Ryan and Jackie were standing on the bank of a stream, spear fishing in the shallow water when they heard the gunshots. They both turned and gazed at the large grove of rattan palms stretching back into the rainforest.

"Those shots came from behind those trees," Ryan said. "What do you think, hunters?"

"That or poachers. If they are, we're in serious trouble."

"What do you want to do? They could be our only way out of the jungle."

"I guess we have to go see."

"I agree."

They made their way through the trees, stepping around brown fronds that had fallen on the ground. Each palm tree had a straw-like skirt of dead fronds around its lower trunk.

Soon, they heard voices and crept silently over to a hedgerow where they wouldn't be seen. Ryan and Jackie crouched down and peered through the leaves.

"I don't believe it." Ryan stood up, grabbed Jackie's hand, and they pushed through the shrubs.

"Oh my God!" Wanda yelled when she saw Ryan running toward her. They embraced and Ryan could tell his mother was crying.

Jackie ran over to James and Kathy and the three hugged.

Ignacio had a big smile on his face and clapped his hands.

Frank came over and put his arm around Ryan and gave him a big squeeze.

"I can't believe you guys came looking for us," Ryan said.

"Ryan, you're my son," Wanda said, declaring that it was her duty as a mother and she'd do anything in the world for him.

"How did you know where to find us?"

"Let's just say Ignacio and Frank are good trackers," Wanda said. She looked over at Frank and he smiled back.

Jackie came over, followed by James and Kathy.

"So, we got your text about poor Miles," Frank said.

"We tried to revive him with CPR but it didn't work," Ryan said.

"Ryan saved my life," Jackie said. "Twice."

"Good for you, son," Frank said. "So what happened to Ben?"

"Don't know," Ryan said. "When our plane crashed into the river, he was the first to get out, but we never saw him after that. He must have drowned."

"Well, you're safe now," Wanda said. "Looks like you two made a pretty good team."

"Yeah, I guess we did," Ryan said and smiled at Jackie.

Ryan saw the humongous dead spider. "Jackie, check that out."

"So that's what you were shooting at," Jackie said, and walked over with Ryan to get a closer look. That's when they saw the man pinned under the giant spider's body.

Ryan turned to Frank, "Is he dead?"

Frank nodded his head.

"We had a similar encounter," Jackie said.

"Oh, and what was that?" Wanda asked.

"A giant praying mantis."

"Yeah, it was as tall as me," Ryan said. "It tried coming at us but when it saw we meant business it flew off."

"I don't get it," Wanda said. "You look around, there're normal-sized insects everywhere, so why the giant ones?"

"That's a good question," Frank said.

"Do you think it might have something to do with the earthquakes?" Wanda asked.

"What, like maybe these creatures were trapped underground and suddenly they're free? I doubt it."

"What if it was a radioactive meteor?" Ryan said. "You know, like in *Slither*."

"Don't forget *The Blob*," Jackie added.

"Sounds like you guys have been watching too many movies," Frank said. "Whatever it is that's causing these mutations, let's just hope that we don't have to deal with any more."

"Well, I don't see any reason to just stand around," Wanda said. "Let's get out of here."

"I'm for that," James said.

"Thank God," Kathy piped in.

"So which way?" Ryan asked.

Frank looked down at his wristwatch and then raised his hand with his index finger pointed up. "Wait for it."

Everyone stood quietly and listened.

The siren was faint but it gave them a direction to go.

46

Frank sliced through the ferns and stepped out onto the edge of a towering bamboo forest. The ten-inch diameter stalks had to be a hundred feet tall. The timber was clustered tightly—no more than shoulder-width—leaving just enough space for a person to step through.

"Did you know that a bamboo plant can grow thirty-six inches in a twenty-four-hour period?" James said as he and Kathy admired the grove of pole-like trees.

"Really, wow," Wanda said. She craned her head back, looked up, and fell backward.

Frank caught her. "Careful."

"Sorry, I got a little dizzy."

Ryan, Jackie, and Ignacio gazed at the tan-colored bamboo maze.

"Looks like a tight squeeze," Jackie said.

"We should be able to get through," Frank said. "Plus, we have these." He waggled his machete.

"Bamboo hard wood," Ignacio said, shaking his head.

"Then I guess I won't need this." Frank put the machete away in the sheath strapped to his rucksack.

Frank led the way as they threaded through the giant stalks. As he had the broadest shoulders, it was a given if he could fit, so could the others.

"This must be the most inhospitable place on the planet," Wanda said.

"Well, the conquistadors from the Old World didn't think so, at least not at first," Frank said over his shoulder. "They believed that there were riches galore, gold and treasures ripe for the taking. Then the New World explorers started dropping like flies from dysentery and malaria or were being killed by the so-called savages."

"Can't say I'm surprised."

"Teddy Roosevelt tried taming the Amazon. The only thing it got him was an infected leg and a bad case of malaria. Five years later he was dead."

The forest ahead stretched so far back that the overlapping stalks gave the false impression that there was a solid wall.

Frank could look to the right and the left and each time see the edges of the cane forest, as it was only forty yards across.

Jackie was the first to see them. "Over there."

Frank turned around and saw that everyone was staring in the direction Jackie was looking.

"Tell me those aren't *aphids*?" Wanda said.

"That's what they are," Frank confirmed.

They were purplish-red—and the size of sheep.

James and Kathy murmured something to each other.

Frank was so used to observing them with a magnifying glass or under a high-power microscope. Seeing them this big was amazing. He considered taking a closer look then quickly changed his mind.

"Everyone, keep your voices down," Frank said when he saw another creature walk up behind the small group of docile plant lice.

"My God," Jackie said, trying to contain her astonishment.

The ant was huge—at least three feet tall at its shoulders and six feet long from its claw-like jaws to the tip of its gaster.

With its head down, the giant ant came up behind the last aphid and nudged it forward. The trailing aphid bumped into the others and they moved a few feet before stopping again.

"Did I just see what I thought I saw?" Wanda whispered to Frank.

"You did. Aphids are sometimes called ant cows because certain ants gather them up in herds so they can milk the bugs for honeydew. Some ants don't know when to quit eating and get so bloated they can't walk. Then the honey pot ants become a nice little smorgasbord for the other ants."

"That's disgusting," Wanda said.

"Maybe so, but we have a bigger problem," Frank said, making sure the others could hear him. "That's a bullet ant."

"Are you sure?" James asked.

"Please tell me you're wrong," Kathy said.

"I'm certain."

"Why do they call it a bullet ant?" Wanda asked. "Because of the shape of its head?"

"I wish. No, it's because of its stinger," Frank said, facing Wanda.

"You mean that thing has a stinger?"

"That's right. Normally, bullet ants are only an inch long. Get stung by one that size and it feels like you've just been shot. Hurts like hell for a day or so. I've gotten stung enough times."

"Oh my God, but this one is huge. That would be like..."

"I don't think we want to find out."

"Guys, keep it down, I think it knows we're here," Ryan said.

Frank turned.

The bullet ant was no longer tending to its flock; it was entering the bamboo forest, and it was managing to slip its way through.

"Okay, everyone. Move it," Frank said. He stepped in and around each stalk blocking his way wishing he could run but it was impossible as some of the time he could barely fit between the close-growing timbers.

He looked back and saw everyone else struggling.

The giant ant was having trouble as well, as it couldn't fit its body between some of the stalks.

"Hurry!" Frank yelled when he saw Kathy starting to fall behind. She had snagged her backpack on the knotty edge of a bamboo tree.

"Don't panic," Frank said. "It can't get at you."

Just as Kathy freed her pack, the giant ant used its jaws and bit right through one of the thick stalks. The severed portion of the trunk fell to the ground and the bamboo tree toppled over, crashing against the other trees.

The new opening was enough for the giant ant to wedge through. It came up behind Kathy, gripped her tightly with its legs then curled its abdomen up and jabbed her in the back with its deadly stinger.

She screamed as though she were on fire then went limp as a rag doll.

The bullet ant lifted the dead woman up with its two front legs, and with its jagged-edged mandibles, bit off her head.

"You son of a bitch!" James yelled.

Wanda pulled her sidearm and fired, but it was near impossible to get a good shot with all the bamboo stalks in the way, so the bullet missed.

"No, no..." James dropped to his knees and wept.

"Ryan, get him up. We have to go," Frank said.

The bullet ant had turned and was heading back to where it had left the small band of aphids.

Everyone kept up as Frank dodged through the maze.

"So Frank," Wanda said, staying on his heels. "What the hell is this place? Certainly no world we've ever seen."

"Your guess is as good as mine. Keep running!"

47

As soon as Macky stepped out of the jungle and saw that they were finally back at the resort, he hollered at the top of his lungs, "We made it!"

"Thank God," Ally said. "I never want to do that again."

"What do you mean?" Dillon said. "I got to play with a baby alligator and a baby pig."

"Peccary," Macky corrected.

"Whatever."

"Let's look around and see if we can find Murilo. I sure hope he's not out on the river looking for us."

"I'd feel really bad if he is," Ally said.

They walked onto the resort's grounds and noticed that some of the debris had been cleared away but not all of it.

"It looks like Murilo got some of it done then stopped," Ally said.

"Must have realized we were missing."

"I know he didn't want us to, but I think we should help with getting the resort back in order."

"I agree," Macky said.

"But first, I need a shower."

"I think we all do. You two go ahead. I'm going to look for Murilo. Maybe he's here somewhere."

Ally and Dillon climbed the stairs up to the catwalk and went into their bungalow.

An hour later, Ally and Dillon came out of their room, refreshed but already perspiring despite having just bathed.

Macky was standing on the catwalk, waiting. He was wearing a change of clothes and his hair was damp from his shower.

Ally looked around. "I take it you didn't find Murilo."

"I looked all over," Macky said. "There's no sign of him."

"I wish there was a way we could contact him."

"Guess we'll just have to wait until he comes back. Here, I found these in a storage shed." Macky was holding two wide-brimmed brooms. He handed a broom to Ally.

"Where do we start?"

"Probably works better if we sweep off the catwalks and let everything fall down on the ground. Then we can drag it over to the trees. That was the way Murilo was doing it."

"Makes sense. We don't want to keep going up and down the stairs carrying this junk."

"What am I supposed to do?" Dillon asked.

"It won't hurt you to help," Ally told her younger brother.

"But I'll get dirty."

"Like that's ever stopped you."

"You know, Dillon, after we're done, I think there's some ice cream in the resort's kitchen."

"Really?"

"That's what I'm thinking. So what do you say?"

"Okey dokey," Dillon said. "I'll help."

Ally smiled and patted her brother on the back. "Good job, Dilly. The sooner we're done, the sooner you get ice cream."

She took her broom and began sweeping the debris off the decking while Macky went over to the adjacent catwalk and began clearing off the fallen branches and anything that was dead.

Dillon tagged along behind Ally, kicking whatever Ally had missed over the side.

A short while later, they were down on the ground, collecting debris and making trips to the jungle's edge.

Ally and Dillon were carrying a tree branch together, her at one end, Dillon at the other.

"We're almost there," Ally said, noticing that Dillon was struggling with his end.

She had her back to the jungle and could hear something moving in the underbrush.

Ally turned. "Hold it, Dillon," she said, and dropped her end.

"Hey, we're almost there."

"Quiet."

"But Ally—"

"Shhh!"

Ally stared at the dense foliage. "Macky, is that you?"

There was no reply, only the sound of a large creature moving about.

Ally took a step back and grabbed Dillon's hand. "I think we're done for now. How about we go have that ice cream?"

"I want Rocky Road."

"Sorry, kid. You get what you get."

Ally moved back slowly and when she thought they were close enough to the stairs, she pulled Dillon and they dashed up to the catwalk.

Macky was coming in their direction, the broom handle draped over his shoulder. "You guys done?"

"Yeah, we're done," Ally said. "Let's go get some ice cream."

48

Ryan and Jackie did their best to console James, but he was pretty broken up about Kathy. How would he be able to explain her death to her parents? She had been killed by an ant, which sounded totally ludicrous if not unbelievable.

It was impossible to retrace their footsteps and they had taken a roundabout way returning to the rescue boat. Frank was fairly certain they were going the right way.

Wanda thought they must have taken a wrong turn, especially when they reached a narrow river.

Frank studied the water. It was about fifty yards to the opposite bank. He had no idea how deep it was or if they could even wade across. "I'm pretty certain this is the way."

"Are you sure? We never crossed a river before," Wanda said. "That I would remember."

"Probably due to the last rain we had. Tributaries get clogged and get rerouted and before you know it, the floodwaters have formed another river. Which is probably what happened here."

Ignacio stood next to Frank and gazed out over the water.

"What do you think?" Frank asked the resort guide. "Think we can get across?"

"Maybe over there," Ignacio said, pointing to the narrowest point where the tops of submerged bushes were sticking out of the water. "Shallower there."

"Good eye, Ignacio. Come on everyone. That's where we're crossing."

Frank went over and stood at the water's edge. Wanda was right behind him, then Ryan and Jackie, James, and Ignacio taking up the rear.

Stepping into the water, Frank took his time as he tested the river's bottom. His boots came down on jumbled rocks. He was thankful that it wasn't boggy, which would make the crossing impossible, as their boots would get stuck in the mud.

"The bottom's pretty firm," Frank said over his shoulder and waved for Wanda to follow him.

One at a time, the rest of the group entered the water single file and followed Frank. The ones with weapons held their firearms over their heads so they wouldn't get wet.

By the time Frank got halfway across, he was up to his chest. He looked back at Wanda, who was nearly up to her chin.

"I hope this is as deep as it gets," Wanda said.

Frank took another step and felt the sole of his boot hit a slight incline. "It's sloping back up," he assured everyone.

Wanda turned her head and looked down the river. "Frank! What the hell is that?"

Frank glanced in that direction.

"That can't be right," Ryan said, spotting the triangular shape knifing through the surface.

"Oh my God," Jackie shouted. "There's another one."

"And more over there!" James yelled.

Frank counted seven shark fins. "Hurry, we have to get out of the water."

"They can't be sharks," Wanda said as she scrambled behind her husband.

"They're bull sharks."

"But I thought sharks only lived in the ocean."

"Not these. They thrive in freshwater."

The lead shark came in first, its bull-shaped body visible even under the brackish water. Frank aimed his rifle and fired, striking the bull shark in the back. The massive fish took an evasive turn and disappeared under the water.

Everyone began splashing as they pushed through the water to get to the other side, the vibrations only causing the four-hundred-pound sharks, some of them ten feet long, to go into a feeding frenzy.

Frank made it up, reached back, and pulled Wanda onto the shore.

Ryan and Jackie were the next ones out of the water. Ryan extended his hand and helped James out.

But Ignacio wasn't so lucky. Two of the sharks had cut him off and had butted him with their snouts while another one came from behind and grabbed hold of his leg.

Ignacio screamed as the sharks converged and ripped at his body. Their tails thrashed in the water as they pulled him under. Massive gouts of blood bubbled to the surface.

There was nothing any of them could do but watch the horror. And even that was too much to bear.

"What is it about this damn jungle?" Wanda said to Frank. He could tell she was royally pissed.

"What do you mean?"

"I mean really, freshwater sharks?" she growled. "What, it thinks it can just keep changing the rules?"

"I'm afraid so," Frank said.

49

Ever since leaving the river and hiking for more than three hours, Frank hadn't been able to stop thinking about Ignacio's tragic death and the giant bullet ant that had killed Kathy. And why had there been only one ant? Ants were social and generally traveled in numbers, especially when they were scouting for food to bring back to the colony. He wondered how the colony would react when the lone ant dragged in Kathy's mutilated body.

"Frank?"

He felt a hand on his shoulder.

"Frank!"

"Huh?" He turned around and saw Wanda staring at him with a puzzled look.

"I've been calling your name but you just keep walking."

"Sorry, I was just..."

"Kathy and Ignacio, I know. Can we take a little break?"

"Sure." Frank stopped and signaled to the others to take a short rest. He took off his pack and found a place to sit. Jackie sat with James, as he was still distraught over Kathy's vicious death. Ryan came over and sat next to his mother.

"Do you think we'll see more of those giant ants?" Ryan asked Frank.

"I don't know."

"So what would be the best way to kill them, if we were attacked?"

"A big can of Raid," Wanda said.

"A very big can." Frank smiled then let his face go somber. "No, seriously, it's good to know your opponent. Ask any fighter that goes into the ring. Ants have the advantage over us as they have exoskeletons and very sharp mandibles. They have an extremely acute sense of smell, touch, and taste and communicate by releasing pheromones. You can't stab them in the lungs because they don't have any. They breathe through tiny holes in their exoskeletons called spiracles."

"Okay, we can rule that one out," Ryan said.

"Forget about puncturing a main artery. They don't have veins like us; blood just flows freely through their bodies."

"Yeah, okay."

"They have a long tube that pumps blood through their bodies and a single nerve that controls their motor functions. Sever those, you might get lucky."

"You make them sound invincible," Wanda said.

"They'd be a formidable opponent, there's no mistaking that."

"What if you shoot them in the head?" Wanda asked.

"It might do the trick. You could blind them, but don't forget they have feelers and could still find you. If you want a sure-fire way to kill one that size, I would suggest severing the petiole."

"What's that?"

"Well, an ant is made up of a head then a body segment called the thorax, where the legs are attached. Then there's the tiny waist called the petiole, which connects the gaster containing the stomachs and the stinger. Cut through the petiole, say with a machete—that would definitely kill it."

"That's good to know," Wanda said.

"I think we've rested enough. We better push on." Frank stood and slung his pack over his shoulder.

He led the way and they forged through the jungle.

50

When Ben woke up he had no idea how long he had been unconscious. He could see a narrow beam of sunlight shining up above. The back of his head throbbed as he sat up. He reached back and felt dried blood matted in his hair.

Slowly, he got to his feet. At first he thought he was in a pit, maybe dug by the pigmies and used for trapping wild game. If that had been true, there would have been sharp stakes pointing upward to impale whatever fell in.

Thankfully that wasn't the case.

As he felt around, he realized that he had fallen into an underground crevice most likely caused by a seismic shift or natural erosion.

He half-expected to see his pursuers standing up on the rim of the hole, ready to throw their spears down at him. Even though he was maybe fifteen feet down, there were exposed tree roots and vines on the dirt walls that he could use to help him climb out.

Ben grabbed hold of a thick vine and hoisted himself up. He stepped on a gnarly root and then another and climbed hand over hand until he finally reached the rim.

Before climbing all the way out, he took a moment to glance around to make sure the pigmies weren't still around. For all he knew, they were biding their time, knowing it would be easier if he unwittingly climbed out rather than having to haul him up.

He was disoriented and had lost all sense of direction. The last thing he wanted to do was wander aimlessly and end up right back at the headhunters' village.

Hi everybody, remember me?

The way his head continued to throb, he was certain he had suffered a concussion.

He listened for a moment to the sounds of the jungle, trying to get his bearings.

That's when he heard what he believed to be the distant roar of a waterfall.

51

Frank heard whispers behind him and turned to Wanda, who was speaking with Ryan in a low voice. "What is it?" he asked. He noticed that Ryan, James, and Jackie were glancing nervously over their shoulders.

"We're being followed," Wanda said.

Frank stopped and peered through the heavy foliage. He saw something move in the shadows. Then other shapes darted from one tree trunk to another.

A small, naked man stepped out between the umbrage.

"My God, that's a pigmy," Jackie said.

The Indian had no weapons and he was smiling.

"He looks friendly enough," Ryan said.

Soon, more naked pigmies appeared and gathered around Frank and the others.

Some of the men had spears but they didn't appear to be hostile. There were fifteen or so and they were all grinning and chattering in their native tongue.

One of the pigmies reached out for Wanda's pack.

"Don't give it to him," Frank said. "Be firm but don't offend him."

Wanda shook her head and held on tightly to the strap of her rucksack.

"Give them a big grin and let's keep moving."

But as soon as Frank took a few steps, the pigmies rushed in front of him and blocked his way. He cradled his rifle in the crook of his arm and gave them a stern look.

"There're more of them hiding back in the trees," Jackie said.

"Yeah, I see them," Ryan said. "They've got bows and arrows."

"That's not all they have," James said. "Look what they're wearing around their waists."

"What, those pouches?" Ryan said.

"Oh God, those are shrunken heads!" Jackie cried out.

Frank gazed through the trees. "Jesus, they're damn headhunters."

The pigmies must have sensed that the jig was up because the smiles quickly left their faces.

"Run!" Frank leveled his rifle and fired down the middle, striking down two of the warriors. He used the butt stock and struck one across the bridge of the nose.

Wanda was right behind Frank, aiming the Browning and picking off a couple more of the natives.

Arrows whished out of the trees like flying daggers.

Ryan and Jackie ran and swung their machetes to scare them back, one pigmy losing a hand when he tried to grab for Jackie.

James blasted a pigmy with his shotgun. He killed another man, emptying the chamber. Two headhunters came at him with their spears.

There was no time to reload.

Fighting their way through the horde, Frank looked over his shoulder and saw James was separated from the group.

The natives were yelling triumphantly, shaking their spears.

James was struck in the back with an arrow. He reached back and was hit in the shoulder and dropped the shotgun. The headhunters were closing in around him.

Frank wanted to go back for James, but he knew it was useless. The arrows were likely poisoned-tipped which meant James was already dying. He couldn't risk Wanda, Ryan, and Jackie getting killed.

So he yelled, "Keep running!" and they bolted through the trees.

52

James plucked the arrow out of his shoulder as one of the pigmies came at him with a spear. He sidestepped his attacker and drove the tip of the arrow into the Indian's face. The man screamed and dropped his spear, grasping the shaft embedded in his eye socket.

Unable to reach the arrow in his back, James leaned over and picked the spear off the ground. He wielded the lance at his assailants, jabbing at the closest ones.

Looking over their heads, James saw the other pigmies armed with bows, aiming their arrows at him. He knew it was impossible to get through the throng and try and catch up with Jackie and the others.

So he chose the path of less resistance and charged into the trees. He could hear them chasing after him. He was in good shape, jogging most days, so he was able to distance himself quickly from the smaller men, though he knew they were better conditioned for endurance being hunters and stalking their prey for long durations.

He'd been running for more than fifteen minutes when he heard a cry behind him that sounded like one of his pursuers had injured themselves. He kept pushing himself, and a minute later, heard another scream.

He came to a halt for a quick breather. He listened for footfalls, but didn't hear anyone coming. Had he lost them? He glanced at his shoulder and saw the blood leaking out of the wound and dripping down his side.

James managed to get his fingers around the shaft of the arrow in his back and slowly pulled it out. He could feel hot blood seeping down the small of his back. He was certain that neither of the arrows had been tipped with poison as he would have already have felt the affects. But he did need to stop the bleeding.

Walking further on, he finally came across a tree that would suit his purpose. He took out his knife and carved into the bark. A thick, red sap oozed out, what was commonly called dragon's blood. He applied the latex, which acted as liquid bandages and would dry quickly and seal the wounds.

He kept listening for the headhunters, but they seemed to have given up looking for him, which struck him as odd. Why hadn't they followed him? Certainly they could have easily tracked him down. Rather than dwell on it, he decided to continue on and hopefully meet up with Jackie and the others.

But after another hour of combing through the jungle, he realized he had no idea if he was even going the right way.

One thing he had noticed was the plant life seemed to be getting increasingly larger.

Especially when he saw humongous soursop fruit hanging from some of the tree branches. He spotted woody vine cat's claws growing in abundance. These plants could also be found in other parts of the Amazon and were used extensively for treating an assortment of aliments. He recognized other plant types, many of which were also used medicinally.

James stopped at the edge of a floral glen. He could smell wonderful fragrances.

The meadow was lush with thousands of brightly colored flowers. He had never seen anything like it before, not even in the Royal Botanic Gardens he once had an opportunity to visit, and doubted if there was such a sight anywhere in the entire world.

It was like he might imagine the Garden of Eden.

Many of the long-stemmed flowers were taller than James and seemed to be looking down at him with their blank pollen faces haloed with brilliant petals.

Awestruck, James entered the splendorous garden. Each plant was marvelous to behold—the many colored orchids, birds-of-paradise, the lilies, and tulips.

But as he trekked through the tropical wonderland, the sweetness of the air diminished.

He began to notice pitcher plants, just a few at first then more as he went.

And then he saw it.

The most magnificent flower he had ever seen. Each petal was a different hue and blended into the next petal in a pinwheel of rainbow colors.

He remembered Frank telling them about Raymond Trodderman's journal and its mention of a spectacular flower that could be the cure for cancer. A flower that, once you saw it, you would know to be the one.

James knew he had found such a flower.

He had to get a specimen. Then try and catch up with the others. Once they were back home he'd lay claim to his discovery. Write a scientific article. Get a patent so as not to get ripped off by the pharmaceutical company that would mass-produce the remedy at an affordable cost—and still make him a billionaire a hundred times over.

James stepped onto a massive red frond at the base of the flower's stem that stood over his head about half the height of a streetlamp. He took his knife and was about to saw through the thick stem to cut down the flower when the giant leaf he was standing on suddenly rose up on both sides and snapped closed, trapping him inside.

He looked up and saw interlocking thorns clasped together. Trigger hairs.

That's when he suddenly realized he had walked into a colossal Venus flytrap—or, more accurately, *mantrap*.

James drove his blade into the thick skin of the giant plant. He tried slicing downward but the wall of the plant was too thick and it was like trying to cut through a leather hide with a plastic knife.

He pushed against one wall hoping to open up the carnivorous plant, but the sides were locked in place. He pulled his hands away when a sticky secretion began to seep out of the plant's pores and trickle down the walls.

James looked down and saw he was standing in a pool of the stuff and it was actually eating through the leather of his boots.

An orifice gradually opened up under him and he began to inch down.

He screamed, knowing his fate, and the torturous pain he would suffer while still alive before being completely dissolved into plant food.

53

Frank knew there was no point in trying to outrun the headhunters. The pigmies were acclimated to the extreme heat and the harsh conditions of the brutal jungle and could no doubt run marathons around them and still not break a sweat.

Sooner or later, they would have to make a stand and fight. He knew he had to decide, and quickly, before they were too exhausted to defend themselves against the murderous barbarians.

"How much farther?" Wanda yelled in between raspy breaths.

Frank saw a break in the trees up ahead and the rock face of a granite hillock. If they were able to get up that, they'd have the advantage of high ground and might be able to fend off their pursuers and possibly end the chase.

"If we can get up there, maybe we'll have a chance."

But then he came to a crashing halt when a giant bullet ant stepped in his path. It was the same size as the one that had killed Kathy—hell, for all he knew it was the same creature—and it wasn't alone. Six more stepped out of the bushes.

Frank prayed they were only scouts and not the prelude of an army from the colony.

He looked over his shoulder and saw Wanda, Ryan, and Jackie stop behind him with questioning expressions on their faces. He could also see the mob of pigmies running straight for them and guessed they hadn't yet seen the monstrous ants only twenty yards away.

Wanda, Ryan, and Jackie saw the giant ants.

"What do we do?" Wanda said.

"Everyone turn and stand shoulder to shoulder. So they can't see the ants."

The four of them turned and faced the charging pigmies, fifty feet away and closing.

"Wait for it," Frank told the others.

The pigmies yelled a war cry and shook their spears as they ran.

Frank heard movement behind them, which meant the ants were advancing, most likely drawn to the sound of the trampling Indians.

"Now?" Ryan asked anxiously.

"Wait."

The headhunters were only fifteen feet away and were coming fast.

"Now!" Frank and Wanda dove into the bushes to their left while Ryan and Jackie catapulted into the shrubs on the right.

The pigmy horde dashed right down the middle, straight into the jaws of the giant bullet ants. The Indians jabbed frantically with their spears, but the ants were relentless, snapping their hacksaw mandibles and severing limbs. Every time a pigmy tried to flee, an ant would pounce and impale him with its stinger, injecting its deadly venom.

Battle cries soon became screams of agony.

The blood splatter on the surrounding greenery and the ground looked like a Jackson Pollock drip painting with all the body parts and viscous gore.

The ants began to busily collect food scraps for the return trip to the colony.

Frank and Wanda crept through the brush. Once they were far enough away, Frank stood up and glanced around for Ryan and Jackie. He didn't have to look for long; Ryan and Jackie had doubled back and had been following them.

"Let's get out of here," Frank said. "Before those damn things come looking for us."

54

Ben continued to follow the sound of the waterfalls and finally broke through the trees onto a ledge. He looked down at the white water cascading down off a sheer cliff wall. It reminded him of the time he and Kathy had taken a trip to Niagara Falls where the powerful water crashing to the rocks below created a billowing mist.

He looked across the gorge and saw another river discharging over the break into a lagoon. The overflow poured down the rocks into the rapids that snaked around a bend and disappeared in the endless rainforest.

Ben glanced to his right.

Five figures were standing only fifty feet away. The pigmy warriors were captivated by the tremendous display of power—the waterfalls a symbol of a great spirit.

One of the pigmies turned. Once he saw Ben he immediately yelled and pointed his spear. The man standing next to him, strung an arrow in his bow, pulled back and released the arrow.

Ben ducked as the arrow zipped over his right shoulder.

The headhunters charged down the boulders, jumping over the rocks.

A pigmy threw his spear, which would have hit its mark if Ben hadn't stepped out of the way in the nick of time.

Ben picked up a rock and threw it but it sailed over their heads.

The savages stopped running and slowly advanced on Ben. Twenty feet away, they formed a half circle and assumed menacing poses to intimidate him.

Ben looked back and realized they were backing him onto a ledge, leaving him nowhere to run. His heels were almost to the edge. He was no match against the fierce warriors.

One more step and he would no longer have to fear the diabolical things they had in store for him.

Suddenly, he was aware of the sound of an approaching turbo engine as he was buffeted by a strong wind, which almost blew him off the edge.

A military army-green gunship appeared over the treetops. Ben could see a gunner wearing a helmet and camouflage fatigues, crouched in the opened side door. The soldier fired a short burst from his fifty-caliber machinegun.

A steady barrage of bullets pocked the rocks, spitting up tiny chunks in a straight line, and strafed the ground in front of the headhunters. The pigmies screamed, turned tail, and ran for the jungle.

Ben waved his arms.

The helicopter hovered and a cable was lowered.

Ben grabbed the swaying line, careful not to over-extend his reach and fall off the ledge. He slipped the adjustable harness strap over his head, and around his chest, cinching it tight. He signaled he was ready.

His feet left the ground and he was hoisted up.

The gunner grabbed his hand and pulled him inside the helicopter.

"Thank God you guys showed up when you did," Ben said appreciatively.

"Are you the pilot?" the soldier yelled so he could be heard over the din of the whirlybird's engine.

"Pilot? No," Ben shouted.

"You're not Miles Gifford?"

"No, I was one of the passengers," Ben said. He sat on a rigid seat next to the sliding door and buckled the seatbelt. "They're all dead. How did you find me?"

The gunner stuck his gloved fist out the opening and pointed his thumb down.

They were flying just above the falls.

Ben could see the outline of the mangled floatplane just beneath the surface of the lagoon.

"We picked up your distress beacon."

Ben smiled and closed his eyes, never so happy to be alive.

55

Even Frank was exhausted when they finally reached the rescue boat. It just so happened Enzo had just sounded the siren so there were spooked birds overhead, flying in all directions in the twilight sky. It would be dark soon.

Wanda stumbled across the sand and leaned against the bow's hull. "I've never been so glad to see this beautiful boat," she said and patted the tire bumper.

Ryan and Jackie went over and climbed aboard.

Enzo stepped out of the pilothouse and gave everyone a welcoming smile. He looked past the couple and saw only Frank and Wanda.

Frank saw the puzzled expression on his face and shook his head. "I'm sorry but Ignacio is dead. So are Ben, James, and Kathy."

Enzo didn't seem to react to the bad news one way or the other, which really didn't surprise Frank. He figured Enzo and Ignacio either had an employee-boss relationship and were not close friends, or Enzo accepted death as just another aspect of living in the dangerous jungle and considered it just a way of life.

"Ryan, help your mom so I can push us off," Frank said.

Wanda walked wearily down the length of the boat. She raised her hand and Ryan hauled her up on the aft deck.

Enzo started one of the outboards. Frank reached up and placed his rifle on the fore deck. He took off his rucksack and tossed it up. "Okay, I'm ready!"

Frank put his shoulder into it and pushed the bow while Enzo reversed the engine.

The front of the rescue boat started to slip off the sandy shore and edged into the water. Frank ran alongside and gripped the gunwale. Ryan grabbed him by the arm and pulled him onto the deck.

"Wouldn't we make better time if we used both outboards?" Ryan asked.

"I think Enzo wants to conserve on gas," Frank explained. "It's a long haul back."

"That makes sense."

"Besides, we can make pretty good time on just one engine."

Enzo gunned the motor and steered down the middle of the river.

Ryan and Jackie went inside the cabin of the pilothouse to relax while Frank and Wanda went around to the fore deck to watch the sun slowly set in the jagged horizon of treetops.

"I can't believe we did it," Wanda said, misty-eyed. "I can't believe we actually found them."

Frank put his arm around Wanda's shoulders. "Maybe we should consider starting our own jungle rescue service?"

"I don't think so," Wanda replied, and gave him a weary look.

"Hey, with the peanuts they pay us, might be a good way to pick up some extra cash."

"Not going to happen."

"Hmmm. Too bad."

"Just shut up and kiss me."

Frank didn't say another word and did as he was told.

***

In all fairness, Frank decided Ryan and he would help Enzo and take one-hour shifts at the helm while Wanda and Jackie got some much-needed rest. They'd been traveling on the river for almost six hours when the two front halogen lights went out.

Ryan was at the helm and abruptly stopped the boat.

Without the powerful spotlights it was too risky navigating with only the dim moonlight that seemed to come and go obscured by the dark clouds accumulating for the next tropical rainstorm.

"Enzo, what's happened to the lights?" Frank asked, looking up at the tall masts.

"Corroded lamps," Enzo replied. He was already inside the pilothouse, rummaging through a locker. He found two packages and carried both out to the aft deck.

"Here, let me help you with those." Frank took a package and put it under his arm. He slit open the wrapping on the other package and removed the lamp. He followed Enzo to the front of the boat.

Enzo went up the ladder to the cabin roof. Frank followed right behind. Being a natural climber, Enzo shimmed up the ten-foot mast on the portside. Once he reached the top, he swung open a mesh screen and removed the lamp. He tossed the burned-out lamp down to Frank and started wiping out any rust that might have formed in the socket.

A light shone in Frank's face.

"Thought I could help," Wanda said, diverting the beam of her flashlight as she climbed to the top of the ladder.

"Thanks, we could use some light." Frank looked up and saw Enzo had finished cleaning the socket and was waiting. "What, you want me to toss it up?"

Enzo nodded.

"Okay, but—"

"Do you hear that?" Wanda said.

Frank had heard it, too.

Like thousands of dry leaves rustling in the trees. Only this sound was coming down the middle of the river; and it was heading straight for the boat.

"Take cover!" Frank yelled. He grabbed Wanda and they lay face down on the cabin roof, covering their heads with their hands.

Frank peered through the crook of his arm and saw nothing but a frenzy of small bodies with flapping wings. There had to be thousands of them.

"What are they?" Wanda yelled over the screeching and the beating wings.

"Vampire bats!" Frank shouted back. He heard a scream down below. It was Jackie. He could feel the vibration of the bats battering themselves against the bulkheads down inside the pilothouse.

Frank looked up and saw Enzo's head and right shoulder. The rest of him was covered with clinging bats. He was holding on with one hand and trying to swat them off of his body and looked like he would fall at any moment.

"Frank, the damn things are biting me!" Wanda shouted.

He looked over and saw Wanda's back was covered and they were walking up her pant legs and using their tiny claws on the edge of their parchment-thin wings to grab hold. He could see their ugly faces as they opened their mouths to nip at Wanda.

"Get off, you..." Frank got up on his knees and began slapping the bats off of Wanda.

But that only seemed to rile them up more. The nasty creatures wrapped their wings around his hands and bit at his fingers like they were a nighttime snack.

They flew at his face.

Then came the steady blare of the high shrill emergency siren.

Mounted on the pilothouse roof, the horn was ear piercing but Frank loved it because it was messing with the vampire's echolocation and causing them to disband and fly off in every direction.

Once the bats had cleared the rooftop, Frank went over and leaned his head down so he could see into the window of the pilothouse. The bats inside were getting their bearings and flying out of the rear doorway. He could see about thirty dead bats on the deck that had collided into the pilothouse.

Jackie stepped out and looked up at Frank. "It was Ryan's idea to sound the siren."

"Tell him good job. It worked." Frank turned and saw Wanda standing up. "You okay?" he asked.

"Damn little bloodsuckers."

"Actually, after they bite you, they're more like little blood lickers."

"I need help up here," Enzo said, still clinging to the mast. There were tiny wet blotches of blood on the back of his t-shirt.

"Sorry," Frank said. "Wanda, we'll need your flashlight again."

"Sure thing." She trained the beam near the top of the mast.

Frank tossed Enzo a new lamp. Enzo caught it with one hand and shoved it into the light housing. He slid down, crossed the roof, and climbed up the other mast. He tossed down the dead lamp and Frank threw up the replacement.

Enzo descended the pole and headed down the ladder to the rear door of the cabin.

"Wanda, we need to tend to everyone's bites and make sure they're disinfected. Enzo got bitten up pretty good. I'll take his turn at the helm."

Wanda just stood there staring at him.

"What?"

"Oh, I don't know. I can't help thinking...what the hell could possibly happen next?"

56

Ryan was too keyed up to sleep after the ordeal with the vampire bats and decided to hang out on the aft deck as it was cooler outside. The humidity had to be off the charts, especially inside the pilothouse. Despite only using one outboard motor, the rescue boat was moving at a good clip and offered a nice breeze to anyone on deck.

He heard the rear door open and was glad to see Jackie stepping out of the cabin.

"It's like a sweatbox in there," she said. "Great time for the air conditioning to crap out."

"How's my mom doing?"

"She and Frank are taking a nap."

"I'm thinking of sleeping out here," Ryan said.

"Who's going to relieve Enzo?"

"I told him I would. I still have another forty-five minutes."

Ryan leaned against the gunwale and put his arm around the small of Jackie's back. He could feel her body press up against him.

She looked beautiful in the moonlight.

He couldn't have picked a better setting for a first kiss; standing under the stars while taking a romantic boat ride through the jungle.

They were cruising under a dense canopy of tree limbs extending over the water.

He leaned in and puckered up while Jackie gazed in to his eyes and opened her mouth slightly. Ryan closed his eyes for the special moment.

"Ahhh," Jackie gagged.

Ryan opened his eyes and pulled his head back. "What is it? What's wrong?"

"A gnat flew into my mouth. Aghh, damn thing's stuck in my throat."

"Hold on, I'll get you some water." Ryan dashed into the cabin. He tried not to wake up his mother or Frank and stepped over to the portable water jug. He opened the spigot, poured water into a cup, and went back outside.

"Here this should..." Ryan stopped when he saw Jackie was gone. He went over to the portside of the boat and looked up the side of the pilothouse but she was nowhere to be seen. He went around the rear of the cabin and looked up the starboard side; still no Jackie.

"Jackie?"

No answer.

That's when he realized she must have fallen off the boat.

Ryan flew into the pilothouse. "Stop the boat! Stop the boat!"

Frank and Wanda woke and sat up on the bench seats.

"What is it?" Frank said.

"Jackie's fallen overboard," Ryan shouted.

Enzo immediately shut down the outboard motor.

"We have to go back!"

"Enzo, reverse the engine. But do it slow," Frank ordered.

Ryan ran back outside and leaned out over the transom. Enzo had directed the aft spotlights to shine on the water behind the boat.

Frank and Wanda stood on either side of Ryan, shining their flashlights into the water.

"Take it nice and slow!" Frank hollered so Enzo could hear him.

The underwater propeller churned up the water as the boat backed up the river.

"Do you see her?" Ryan shouted frantically.

"No, son," Wanda said, panning her light on the water's surface. "It's so murky, I can't see a thing."

The boat started to go back under the dense overhang of tree branches.

Ryan looked up and saw Jackie's boot protruding out of the leaves. "Up there! She's up in the trees!"

Frank shined his flashlight in the foliage.

"My God, how did she get up there?" Wanda said.

"I can see her," Frank said. "Wanda, do you see it?"

Wanda looked up and followed the beam of light from Frank's flashlight. "I do." She drew the nine-millimeter Browning, aimed, and fired three shots.

"Everybody look out," Frank warned as something heavy crashed down through the branches.

The boa constrictor slammed down on the deck with Jackie still coiled in its death grip.

Wanda stepped up and shot the snake in the head.

Ryan and Frank lifted the enormous anaconda and unraveled its thick body off of Jackie.

"Jackie, can you hear me?" Ryan said, leaning down to see if she was still breathing. He was only inches away from her face when she opened her eyes.

"Ryan?"

"Thank God."

Jackie looked over at the dead snake, which if straightened out, would have stretched to twenty feet long. "As soon as you left, it dropped its tail down, and pulled me up."

Frank turned and shouted, "It's okay, Enzo, we have her."

Enzo waved. He stopped the boat then thrust the throttle forward.

Jackie looked up at Ryan and gave him a smile. "So, where's my water?"

"Coming right up. Just do me a favor—don't go anywhere."

"Deal."

57

"There it is," Ryan said, as the rescue boat came around the bend and everyone saw the welcoming sight of the boat dock at the Black Caiman Jungle Lodge and Resort.

A man was standing at the end of the pier.

"Oh my God, is that Ben?" Jackie said.

"It sure is," Ryan replied. "How the heck did he get here?"

Frank stood at the bow and tossed the mooring line out on the wharf. Ben grabbed the end and wrapped one turn around a cleat then took out the slack as the boat came alongside the pier.

"We thought you were dead," Ryan said.

"I can't believe you guys made it," Ben replied.

Enzo turned off the outboard engine and came out of the pilothouse and joined Wanda on the aft deck.

"How long have you been back?" Jackie asked Ben.

"I just got here. A Brazilian army chopper found me and dropped me off."

"Thank God you guys are back," Ally yelled, running down the pier with Macky and Dillon to greet them.

Wanda stepped off the boat. She opened her arms and hugged Ally and Dillon.

Enzo looked down the pier. "Where's Murilo?"

"We're not sure," Ally said. "We can't seem to find him."

"Mom, I got to play with baby alligators," Dillon said.

"You what—?"

"I'll tell you later, Mom," Ally said. "It was no big deal, right, Macky?"

"Just another day at the petting zoo."

"So where's James and Kathy?" Ben asked.

"I'm afraid they're dead," Frank said. "Ignacio as well."

"Jesus, what a mess," Ben said. "I guess Ryan told you what happened to Miles?"

"Yeah," Frank said. "So how'd they find you?"

"The floatplane had a distress signal."

"You mean they were looking for you guys the whole time?" Wanda said.

"No, I think they picked up the signal by chance," Ben replied.

"How about we go get cleaned up?" Frank said. "We can share horror stories later."

"I'm for that," Wanda said.

"We do have some good news," Ally said as everyone disembarked the boat and began walking down the pier. "The airport will be opening in a couple of hours."

"Hallelujah," Wanda said joyously.

58

After everyone had showered and put on fresh clothes, they packed up their belongings and gathered in the lobby. A luggage cart was next to the front entrance, loaded with suitcases and duffle bags.

Ryan and Jackie were sitting together on a rattan couch, exchanging email addresses. Ryan didn't have any high hopes his cell phone would even take a charge, let alone work, after what it had been through, but surprisingly it performed just fine.

Dillon glanced through the window and saw a family of spider monkeys outside on the catwalk, scampering down the railing. He looked over at Ally, sitting next to Macky on another couch.

"Ally, can I go play with the monkeys?"

"No," Ally said in a firm tone. "You stay where I can see you."

"Mom?" Dillon whined.

"You heard your sister," Wanda said. She was standing by the counter with Frank, who had a perplexed look on his face.

"What's wrong?" she asked.

"I'm worried about Murilo. Enzo says he's looked just about everywhere but still can't find his brother."

"The river taxi isn't going to be here for another couple of hours."

"We need to help him. These guys put their lives on the line for us. It's the least we can do."

"Ally told me a little bit about what happened here while we were gone," Wanda said.

"Oh, yeah. What was that?"

"Seems Ally, Macky, and Dillon went out in a canoe and the thing capsized. Apparently they got lost in the jungle."

"Seriously?" Frank almost laughed.

"Yeah, well, Ally thinks Murilo went looking for them and never made it back."

"So he might not even be anywhere around here."

"Probably not, but maybe we should take a look for ourselves."

"Let's take Ryan and Jackie with us. Ally and Macky can stay here and watch Dillon. Don't want anybody else getting lost."

Wanda walked over and told Ally their plan. She waved to Ryan and Jackie to come with her and Frank as they walked out of the lobby.

"First thing, let's find Enzo," Frank said. "Tell him we're going to help him find his brother."

"I see him," Ryan said. "He's down there by that clearing."

When they got down to the ground and walked over, they saw a pained look on Enzo's face.

"What is it?" Frank asked.

Enzo didn't say anything, just pointed over his shoulder at the edge of the jungle.

Frank led the way and they pushed through the high grass and low-hanging limbs into the gloomy foliage. They hadn't gone twenty paces when they saw the mutilated body on the leaf-covered ground.

"Looks like he found Murilo," Frank said.

"Oh my God," Wanda said.

"He's been torn to pieces," Ryan said.

The stench was awful, the entrails and chewed flesh smothered with flies.

Jackie covered her nose and mouth with her hand and walked up to the corpse.

"He was attacked by a jaguar," she said. "See the punctures in Murilo's skull. The panther bit into his brain then dragged him into the trees."

"You mean there's a killer jaguar roaming around the resort?" Wanda said.

"Judging by the condition of Murilo's body, the big cat's not finished, which means it can't be too far off."

"Mom! Where are you?" It was Ally's voice.

They left the body and came out into the clearing where Enzo was standing.

Ally and Macky were standing on the catwalk, looking down.

"What's the matter?" Wanda yelled up.

"It's Dillon! He's wandered off and we can't find him anywhere!"

59

"What do you mean, you can't find him?" Wanda yelled as she raced up the steps to the catwalk. Frank was right behind her.

"I was showing Macky something on my phone and when I looked up, he was gone," Ally said, almost crying.

"Don't worry, we'll find him," Frank said. He ran down one of the catwalks, yelling Dillon's name.

"We'll stay down here and look for him," Ryan said. He went in one direction, Jackie the opposite way. Enzo seemed to snap out of it and went looking for the boy.

"Ally, we have to find him, and I mean, now!" Wanda said sternly.

"What is it?"

"We found Murilo's body in the jungle."

"Oh, my God." Ally burst into tears. "He's dead?"

"Jackie says it was a big cat. A jaguar!"

"Dillon! Where are you?" Ally shouted and started running down the catwalk.

Macky came around a corner on a parallel catwalk.

"Have you seen him?" Wanda called out.

"I think he went that way," Macky said, pointing. "Before he snuck off, I know he wanted to go out and play with the monkeys."

Wanda wished she still had the Browning but she had left it on the rescue boat, along with the hunting rifle Frank had been using.

She heard chattering and babbling just up ahead.

Monkey gibberish.

Wanda dashed over the catwalk and stopped short at the head of the stairs that led down to the ground. Dillon was halfway down the steps and he was chasing a small spider monkey.

"Dillon, get back up here on the double!"

But Dillon had his mind set on catching the monkey and there was nothing Wanda could say that would stop him. He scampered down to the last step.

The jaguar stood only ten feet away. The two-hundred-pound panther squatted down and hunched its shoulders ready to spring.

Ryan and Jackie sprinted across the clearing, yelling at the big cat.

Frank raced down another flight of stairs but he was too far away to save the boy.

Wanda charged down the stairs.

Dillon looked up in surprise as the big cat launched into the air.

Then came a loud explosion.

The jaguar landed a foot in front of Dillon. It lay in the dirt with its tongue hanging out and most of its side blown apart.

Enzo stepped out from under the catwalk and opened the breech on his shotgun, expelling the two spent shells.

Wanda gave Enzo a look of gratitude and smiled as everyone rushed over to make sure Dillon hadn't been hurt.

Enzo nodded then walked back into the jungle to be with his brother.

60

Frank turned onto the gravel driveway and before he could put the '56 Chevy into park, the backdoors flung open. Ally and Dillon piled out one side, Ryan out the other. They ran around to the front of the farmhouse and dashed up the porch steps.

"So how was your vacation?" asked Deputy Hank Burns, still in uniform but obviously off duty as his shirt was hanging out and he was holding a can of beer.

"Pretty wild," Ryan said, holding the screen door open for his sister and brother.

"So glad to be out of the jungle," Ally said, stepping into the house.

"It was awesome," Dillon said. He stopped and looked up at the deputy. "And Ryan's got a girlfriend."

"Is that right," Hank said.

"Get a move on, squirt," Ryan said and shooed his little brother through the doorway.

Frank came around the corner of the porch, lugging two suitcases, Wanda right behind him carrying a suitcase and a small duffle bag.

"Here, let me help you with that," Hank said. He put his beer can on the railing and skipped down the steps, grabbing the luggage from Wanda.

"Thanks, Hank. How was house sitting?"

"Well, we didn't burn the place down."

"Thank God for that. Any luck finding a place?"

"Yeah. I'm renting a cottage over by the McDermott Ranch. Means I'll only be ten minutes from the office." Hank put

Wanda's things down on the deck and grabbed his beer off the railing.

"How were the dogs?"

"Winston's been my tagalong buddy, but I think Rochelle really missed Dillon because she hasn't been eating much."

Inside the house, they could hear Dillon yelling, "Girl, I'm home," and his bulldog barked and whined with glee.

A white English bull terrier pushed open the screen door with its nose and scampered over to Wanda. "Did you miss me? Oh, I bet you did," she said and gave Winston a pat on the head.

"You got any more bags you need help with?" Hank asked.

"A few in the trunk, but that's okay, I'll get them in a bit," Frank said.

"Well, if you all don't mind, I think I'll run along. I've got some unpacking of my own at my new place." He took a last pull on his beer, squashed the can on the railing and handed the crumpled metal to Wanda. "See you on Monday."

"Thanks again," Wanda said.

"See you around, Hank," Frank said.

The deputy gave them a wave and climbed in his pickup parked by the mailbox.

Wanda looked over at Frank. "You know what I feel like doing right now?"

"Dinner?"

"Soaking in a nice hot tub."

***

Frank carried the pot roast into the dining room and placed the serving dish in the middle of the table. Wanda was already seated at one end, Ally and Dillon on her right, Ryan on the left. Frank walked by Dillon, gave the boy a pat on the shoulder, and sat at the head of the table.

"This looks wonderful," Frank said, gazing at the beef platter, the steaming bowls of mashed potatoes and green beans, two breadbaskets with hot biscuits, and a gravy boat full of brown gravy.

Once everyone had put food on their plates and eaten most of their meal, Wanda asked the family, "What do we tell people when they ask about our vacation?"

"Well, I'm sure Ally and Dillon will have plenty to share with their friends," Frank said. He looked over at Ryan. "Of course, they don't need to know about everything."

"Do you think you'll ever want to go back there?" Ryan asked Frank.

"Well, I wouldn't mind—"

"I know what you're thinking Frank and you can forget it. We're never setting foot in that jungle ever again."

"But…"

"Never," Wanda said, ending any further discussion on the matter.

"I suppose you're right. Some places are best left alone, I guess."

"Exactly," Wanda said as she took her last bite. "Well, if everyone's done—"

"Oh, before you guys run off, I'd like to share something with all over you," Frank said, reaching in his back pocket.

"Okay," Wanda said, half out of her chair, but sitting back down.

Frank placed a folded brochure on the table.

"And what is that?" Wanda asked suspiciously.

"Well, I thought for our anniversary we could book our next trip," Frank said.

"You better be talking Maui."

"Even better. What do you say to a weeklong safari in Africa? And we can all go!"

Ryan looked at his mother and could tell she was fuming. "I've got some work to do in the barn," he said and excused himself from the table.

"I'll go start the dishwater," Ally said. She stacked a few dishes and hurried into the kitchen.

"Are there lions?" Dillon asked.

"Sure, lots of them."

"I want to go."

"Dillon, go clean your room. We'll have dessert later," Wanda said. She grabbed some dirty dishes off the table and glared at Frank. "You're really something." She stormed off into the kitchen.

"Boy, you sure made Mom mad," Dillon said.

"Better go clean your room," Frank said, but when he saw the downcast look on Dillon's face, he leaned in close and whispered, "But don't worry, we've got a year to wear her down."

THE END

ABOUT THE AUTHOR

Gerry Griffiths lives in San Jose, California, with his family and their five rescue dogs and a cat. He is a Horror Writers Association member, has over thirty published short stories in various anthologies and magazines, as well as a short story collection entitled *Creatures*. He is also the author of three novels, *Silurid*, *Death Crawlers*, and *The Beasts of Stoneclad Mountain*, published by Severed Press.

CHECK OUT OTHER GREAT HORROR NOVELS

BLACK FRIDAY
by Michael Hodges

Jared the kleptomaniac, Chike the unemployed IT guy, Patricia the shopaholic, and Jeff the meth dealer are trapped inside a Chicago supermall on Black Friday. Bridgefield Mall empties during a fire alarm, and most of the shoppers drive off into a strange mist surrounding the mall parking lot. They never return. Chike and his group try calling friends and family, but their smart phones won't work, not even Twitter. As the mist creeps closer, the mall lights flicker and surge. Bulbs shatter and spray glass into the air. Unsettling noises are heard from within the mist, as the meth dealer becomes unhinged and hunts the group within the mall. Cornered by the mist, and hunted from within, Chike and the survivors must fight for their lives while solving the mystery of what happened to Bridgefield Mall. Sometimes, a good sale just isn't worth it.

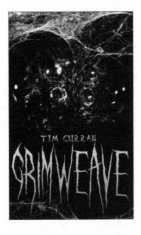

GRIMWEAVE
by Tim Curran

In the deepest, darkest jungles of Indochina, an ancient evil is waiting in a forgotten, primeval valley. It is patient, monstrous, and bloodthirsty. Perfectly adapted to its hot, steaming environment, it strikes silent and stealthy, it chosen prey: human. Now Michael Spiers, a Marine sniper, the only survivor of a previous encounter with the beast, is going after it again. Against his better judgement, he is made part of a Marine Force Recon team that will hunt it down and destroy it.

The hunters are about to become the hunted.

CHECK OUT OTHER GREAT HORROR NOVELS

DEATH CRAWLERS
by **Gerry Griffiths**

Worldwide, there are thought to be 8,000 species of centipede, of which, only 3,000 have been scientifically recorded. The venom of Scolopendra gigantea—the largest of the arthropod genus found in the Amazon rainforest—is so potent that it is fatal to small animals and toxic to humans. But when a cargo plane departs the Amazon region and crashes inside a national park in the United States, much larger and deadlier creatures escape the wreckage to roam wild, reproducing at an astounding rate. Entomologist, Frank Travis solicits small town sheriff Wanda Rafferty's help and together they investigate the crash site. But as a rash of gruesome deaths befalls the townsfolk of Prospect, Frank and Wanda will soon discover how vicious and cunning these new breed of predators can be. Meanwhile, Jake and Nora Carver, and another backpacking couple, are venturing up into the mountainous terrain of the park. If only they knew their fun-filled weekend is about to become a living nightmare.

THE PULLER
by **Michael Hodges**

Matt Kearns has two choices: fight or hide. The creature in the orchard took the rest. Three days ago, he arrived at his favorite place in the world, a remote shack in Michigan's Upper Peninsula. The plan was to mourn his father's death and figure out his life. Now he's fighting for it. An invisible creature has him trapped. Every time Matt tries to flee, he's dragged backwards by an unseen force. Alone and with no hope of rescue, Matt must escape the Puller's reach. But how do you free yourself from something you cannot see?

CHECK OUT OTHER GREAT HORROR NOVELS

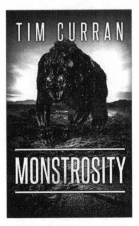

MONSTROSITY
by Tim Curran

The Food. It seeped from the ground, a living, gushing, teratogenic nightmare. It contaminated anything that ate it, causing nature to run wild with horrible mutations, creating massive monstrosities that roam the land destroying towns and cities, feeding on livestock and human beings and one another. Now Frank Bowman, an ordinary farmer with no military skills, must get his children to safety. And that will mean a trip through the contaminated zone of monsters, madmen, and The Food itself. Only a fool would attempt it. Or a man with a mission.

THE SQUIRMING
by Jack Hamlyn

You are their hosts

You are their food.

The parasites came out of nowhere, squirming horrors that enslaved the human race. They turned the population into mindless pack animals, psychotic cannibalistic hordes whose only purpose was to feed them.

Now with the human race teetering at the edge of extinction, extermination teams are fighting back, killing off the parasites and their voracious hosts. Taking them out one by one in violent, bloody encounters.

The future of mankind is at stake.

And time is running out.

66720938R00110

Made in the USA
Lexington, KY
22 August 2017